T'TA PROFESSOR

T'TA PROFESSOR

MANOHAR SHYAM JOSHI

Translated from the Hindi by
IRA PANDE

PENGUIN
VIKING

VIKING

Published by the Penguin Group

Penguin Books India Pvt. Ltd, 11 Community Centre, Panchsheel Park,
New Delhi 110 017, India

Penguin Group (USA) Inc., 375 Hudson Street, New York, New York 10014, USA

Penguin Group (Canada), 90 Eglinton Avenue East, Suite 700, Toronto,
Ontario, M4P 2Y3, Canada (a division of Pearson Penguin Canada Inc.)

Penguin Books Ltd, 80 Strand, London WC2R 0RL, England

Penguin Ireland, 25 St Stephen's Green, Dublin 2, Ireland
(a division of Penguin Books Ltd)

Penguin Group (Australia), 250 Camberwell Road, Camberwell,
Victoria 3124, Australia (a division of Pearson Australia Group Pty Ltd)

Penguin Group (NZ), 67 Apollo Drive, Rosedale, North Shore 0632,
New Zealand (a division of Pearson New Zealand Ltd)

Penguin Group (South Africa) (Pty) Ltd, 24 Sturdee Avenue, Rosebank,
Johannesburg 2196, South Africa

Penguin Books Ltd, Registered Offices: 80 Strand, London WC2R 0RL, England

First published in Hindi as *T'ta Professor* by Kitabghar, India, 1995
First published in Viking by Penguin Books India 2008

Copyright © Bhagwati Joshi 1995, 2008
Translation copyright © Ira Pande 2008

All rights reserved

10 9 8 7 6 5 4 3 2 1

ISBN 9780670082094

This is a work of fiction. Names, characters, places and incidents are either the
product of the author's imagination or are used fictitiously and any resemblance to
any actual person, living or dead, events or locales is entirely coincidental.

Typeset in *Calisto MT* by SÜRYA, New Delhi
Printed at Chaman Offset Printers, New Delhi

6 'Poets must die when they're young and novelists be born only when they're old.' Can't recall where I read that line, or its author's name. God knows who wrote it: a failed middle-aged poet or a successful old novelist. Sounds more like the former, if you ask me. A middle-aged German poet, perhaps, with a bald pate and a malodorous body, whose female admirers peer beyond his beer-bloated, flatulent belly trying to find the young man who wrote romantic lyrics.

Look, successful or not, I am a middle-aged novelist too, and although I may now write to live, I no longer live to write. All the stories I put off writing because I waited for them to mature, have grown old along with me. In fact, they are as close to death as I am now. So what immortality can this dying baggage have?

Mind you, once—very long ago—I dreamt of writing immortal stuff, something that would floor my readers and critics. And perhaps I did write an odd dozen that future generations may read on a bright and sunny or dark and cloudy day. Such readers may pause at a sentence, mark the page ruminatively with a finger or get up to read it aloud to someone else. But when they look out of the window and see the brave new world, they'll probably shake their heads and say to themselves, 'No—anyone I read this to will think I've gone a bit soft in the head. This is for those who value period writing or those nuts who believe in literary immortality and that sort of shit.'

My old world is dying all around me: what is more, even the memories of that world now appear old and tired like me. So...no, I don't believe in anyone's immortality now, least of all in my own. I have virtually given up writing; in fact, I find now that I can't even muster up the desire to read anything written by someone else. I often find it difficult now to remember myself as the young writer who once had stories bubbling up inside him as spontaneously as laughter and tears. Was I the man who once, while drinking a solitary cup of tea in the restaurant behind the University, suddenly burst into laughter and then hastily got up and left before someone thought I had gone mad? Was it me who left, still chuckling over my thoughts, in search of someone with whom to share the reason why I laughed? Someone to whom I could relate an entire plot, while talking and walking at the same time, completely oblivious of the traffic or even the people on the road who turned to stare at me? Was it me who could, at the sound of an old romantic film song, or on reading a line like 'Poets must die young. . .' get a lump in my throat and tears in my eyes? Unable to summon a listener, I'd run then to the bathroom and stare into the mirror over the washbasin at the spectacle of my welling eyes and contorting face and silently relive the story that lay trapped in those tears.

Was that me? Or was it a character in one of my stories?

Whatever the truth, I am no longer that man. Period. I seem to have lost the magic button that created waves of emotion within me, the one that made me laugh and cry without reason. It's all haywire now, so that often I cry when I should laugh and burst into laughter when I should burst into tears. And all those stories that I did not write in my youth have aged and died a little—like me—some outside me, and some within.

However, there were some promising stories that I looked at from time to time, to test their health, as it were. I raged against their ageing as I raged against mine. I have piles of dusty files with several opening chapters written between long gaps. All they seem to me now are mute reminders that both my imagination and handwriting have deteriorated over the years. Among that collection of trash are also some luckless plots that took birth, developed, and died of suffocation in my mind even before they saw ink and paper.

What I am about to write is a requiem for just such a tale.

∾

I had gone to Almora last summer to visit our ancestral home, when I was reminded of this tale by someone (he was actually a character in it) from a moving bus. There I was, standing near a dried-up apricot tree in our home, reflecting on the ancestor who must have planted it, when someone from the road above our home yelled: 'Joshi, Ma'at-saip!'

My startled gaze flew up and I saw a private bus going to Bageshwar that had probably stopped to pick up a passenger from the main road above our house. I traced the voice of my hailer to an old man, who appeared to be smiling at me from one of the windows. I hurried up the terraced fields that led to the road and furiously jogged my brain to recall who he could be. He'd called me 'Ma'at-saip', so I figured he must have some connection with Sunaulidhar village, the only place where I had ever taught in a school. It was also the only time in my entire life when I was called 'Ma'at-saip'—Kumaoni for 'master-sahib'.

I huffed my way up to the road where the bus stood. The old man looked at me from a window and congratulated me on having become such a famous writer. I tried desperately to remember his name and what he must have looked like when he was younger. No luck. So all the while that he talked to me, I schooled my face to wear an expression that said, 'Of course I remember you!' It was only when he talked of how he had been left far behind me in the literary rat race and cursed his own fate that the penny dropped. So this was the junior clerk of the Sunaulidhar school who wrote horrendous romantic verse, I recalled. But no matter how hard I tried, the idiot's name still eluded me.

The driver cranked his old bus into life and as it

lurched forward, the poet yelled, 'Ma'at-saip, won't you write about "T'ta Professor" Khashtivallabh Pant, Dubbul MA?'

I never got a chance to respond. By now the bus had gathered some speed, so when he waved his hand like Khashtivallabh I waved a limp hand foolishly in return, my lips soundlessly mouthing a 't'ta'. I slowly walked down the hill again, still trying to recall the man's name, but although a line of his vile poetry came clearly to me, for the life of me, I could not remember it. Faces have had names erased, and names hover in my head without accompanying faces now. The departing poet must have also often reflected on the frustrations felt by an ageing, creaky brain because he was, after all, a poet: a poet and a junior clerk. Just as I was then a writer: a writer and a temporary schoolmaster.

And all of a sudden I was transported to a time when I lived in a faraway village called Sunaulidhar that had the Himalayas studded on its horizon like a gleaming horseshoe.

I was in rebellion against my family and the tyranny of university examinations those days. I had botched my

MA exam and, after a quarrel at home, landed in the remote village of Sunaulidhar so that my family would not nag me to try and get a government job. For their peace of mind, I'd told them that I would do a 'private' MA but actually all I had wanted to do was to live in a pretty village and write.

The day I went to the school for the first time, I realized that the atmosphere there was pretty loaded. And I mean that in a comical sense. My first encounter was with the headmaster of the school—Shobhan Singh. He objected to my calling him a headmaster and said, call me Principal, please; the 'headmaster' here is one Khashtivallabh Pant, who prefers to be called Professor.

Ah, I thought, chuckling silently. So this little school that had just been promoted to a high school from a middle school had a principal *and* a professor! As he went on about the running feud between himself and Khashtivallabh, the poetic possibilities of the pretty village retreated from my mind before its huge comic potential. Then, to impress me, a graduate from Lucknow University, Shobhan Singh dropped several important names so that I understood how he was no yokel but one of us. What he did not think it necessary to address, however, was the small matter of where I would stay. When the manager of the school had interviewed me in

Almora for the job, he had clearly mentioned that Principal-saip would give me a room in the quarters that had been constructed for him. Principal-saip, on the other hand, suggested that I may use the unfinished storeroom of the school laboratory as my digs and share it with the junior clerk.

So I reached the storeroom of the lab and found the junior clerk addressing an envelope to the editor of *Saraswati* magazine. I introduced myself and gave him the principal's message and asked where I could keep my stuff. He cursed the principal saying, 'He could have let you put your things in the office, couldn't he?'

I let that pass, and asked him, 'Are you a writer?'

'I am a Poet,' he replied petulantly. 'A Poet, understand? Not some writer-viter.'

I told him pleasantly that I was a writer too, and that one of my scientific articles had recently appeared in *Sangam*. Scientific articles can hardly be called writing, he sneered.

'Talk to me of short stories and novels, understand? I am sending my poem to *Saraswati* for publication and have to leave for the post office now.' Then he cast a disdainful eye over my luggage. 'Keep your things here if you must, but I am not going to leave you here alone, understand? There is too much stuff lying here—the

8

lab's, my own. . .If anything goes missing, the shit will break over *my* head,' he said darkly.

I offered to walk with him to the post office for I also had a short story to send to *Sangam* magazine. So we both reached the village bazaar which had all of two shops. The first one belonged to Jeet Singh, who stocked everything from groceries to shoes and clothes, and also doubled as the village post office. The junior clerk had by now worked out that the editor of *Sangam*, Ilachandra Joshi, must be some relative of mine and promptly asked me to put in a word for his poems. I said I would certainly help him with a letter to the editor who, incidentally, was no cousin or relative. However, I did know him. The young man then proceeded to tell me of the nepotism rampant in the literary world, confiding that this was why he always wrote under a pseudonym.

'I always keep clear of all caste biases,' he said virtuously. 'However, if you recommend my work to Ilachandra-ji,' he added slyly, 'he will know I am a brahmin.' Then he hurriedly checked whether I belonged to the same subcaste as the editor. I assured him that neither the editor nor I had any interest in our castes or subcastes.

So we posted our work and, to celebrate the discovery that Sunaulidhar now had two writers, decided to visit the second shop of the village whose owner, Kheem Singh, sold tea, jalebis, pakoras and delicious potato gutkas. I ended up not only paying for this celebration but also listening to the junior clerk's poetic outpourings as well. By now he had unbent sufficiently to pay attention to the problem of my homelessness.

'Here there is no such thing as rooms to rent,' he informed me between noisy slurps of tea. 'Everyone lives in his own house where many generations of a family live together. There *is* one largish house that has place,' he went on, 'but that belongs to "T'ta", Professor Khashtivallabh Pant, and there is no way he will accept you as a tenant because you were appointed by my uncle, Sher Singh, manager of the school board. You see, T'ta hates Sher Singh because when the school was promoted to a high school recently, Sher Singh imported a principal from Nainital instead of giving T'ta the job.'

'Is this Pant some retired professor?' I asked innocently.

'Hah!' he snorted contemptuously. 'He is an ordinary schoolmaster who started his career here when this was a primary school. He wants to become a professor and that is why he has done a dubbul MA—in Hindi and history. Privately. He keeps sending applications to colleges all over but you know how it is: Apply, apply, no reply.'

'So was he upset at not being appointed principal?' I asked.

'Was he not!' the young man continued. 'He really believes that his efforts led to our primary school being promoted to a high school, get it? Now it's true that my uncle, the manager, asked him to write out the applications for him, but that doesn't mean that T'ta was responsible for this happening! Getting all this organized was my uncle's effort—he took the help of his brother-in-law, the forest contractor Pan Singh Bisht, who donated the slush money needed to move the red tape, understand?'

My head was reeling by now and by the end of all this, all I knew was that I was still homeless and would probably end up sleeping under the stars on a bed of pine needles through my stay. When I told the junior clerk as much, his poetic heart was so moved at my plight that he vowed to get me a room and kitchen in T'ta's house. So, armed with a letter from his uncle the manager, he took me to T'ta's place.

T'ta was busy doing some complex yogic exercises and we had to wait a while. He came, glanced through the letter, pointed out several grammatical mistakes and informed us curtly that he was not prepared to share his home with any Tom, Dick or Harry. Ignoring me completely, he then turned to the junior clerk and said that whoever this Mr Joshi-Hoshi may be, his house had no spare room.

'In fact,' he went on, still addressing the junior clerk and studiously avoiding my eyes, 'I want to send a message to your uncle that people like this Joshi person should not be appointed teachers in the school. When the school had a dubbul MA like me to teach the children Hindi and history, what do they mean by hiring a mere graduate like this person to handle maths and science? And that too, a person who shamelessly smokes in the presence of his elders and betters? What kind of ideal is he going to set for our students? Look at him, a mere stripling—how on earth is he going to control the rough and robust village boys?'

We slunk away and the junior clerk placed my predicament before Principal-saip. I had imagined that the principal would be able to persuade the clerk to let me share the storeroom with him but instead I found the junior clerk asking me why I had accepted a position in Sunaulidhar when I had no place of my own in the village.

Slowly, the power dynamics of the school were becoming clear to me: the principal was beholden to the school manager who had got him appointed principal over T'ta. The clerk was the manager's nephew so he had a claim on the principal's support. Thus, his insisting that the principal share his house with me—rather than offering to share his own room—started to make sense.

Eventually, the matter was resolved when the principal decided that Kheem Singh should be told to give Joshi-jyu a room in his 'hotel'.

Kheem Singh was located and, after he was made to see how critically dependent he was on the income from the school's students and teachers, he had no choice but to agree that the storeroom behind his shop would be my lodgings and he'd provide me with my meals. So Kheem Singh shoved aside the sacks of potatoes and firewood to one corner and put in a wooden takht and a table and chair for me. Thus it was that I became the first and only tenant of Kheem Singh's 'hotel'.

I believe he still quotes the five rupees and eleven annas I am supposed to owe him for his contribution to the cause of Hindi literature.

To cut a long story short, I started living in Kheem Singh's 'hotel' and sat on a rickety chair as I composed literature on an even more rickety table. In between, I also swallowed unavoidable doses of the poetic outpourings of the junior clerk, who was delighted that not only had he now access to an account at Kheem Singh's shop, but also that there was a fellow writer who was not averse to poetry and gossip. The main subject of the gossip was T'ta because he was the declared enemy of the junior clerk's uncle, the manager.

One day, as the junior clerk was on his favourite subject, the man in question came to the neighbouring post office-cum-general store and started chatting with the owner, Jeet Singh. The subject of T'ta's declamation was the teachers of today, and every barb was clearly aimed at me.

The junior clerk whispered conspiratorially that T'ta invariably came to Jeet Singh's shop in time for the post from the town because he was scared that someone may read the love letters he received. But who could possibly fall in love with a man like T'ta, I asked my companion.

'Only T'ta knows the answer to that,' the junior clerk shrugged, 'or possibly his lover. All we know is that there is a lover somewhere. The postman tells us that three or four times a year, T'ta gets a letter with the name and address written in a particular hand. Earlier, the postmark was Lahore but after '47, the letters come from Delhi,' he said darkly.

'But it could be a relative, couldn't it?' I said.

'Oh, we know all about his relatives,' he scoffed. 'The old man had an uncle in Lahore once upon a time, and T'ta ran away from his village to study there. But the minute T'ta's gloomy shadow fell on that house, the uncle died of a heart attack. The uncle was an Arya Samaji bachelor so there is no possibility of T'ta having any cousins there.'

At this point, the postman appeared and smilingly handed over an envelope to Professor-saip.

'Look, look,' the junior clerk nudged me, 'look at T'ta's eyes light up. I swear even the old man's nose is twitching, guru,' he giggled. 'Tell me, have you ever seen anyone's eyes light up like that on getting a cousin's letter, huh? Wonder who the Heer of this cartoon Ranjha is! I've often begged the postman to let me steam the letter open. Promised him I'll stick it back exactly as it is but the wretch won't let me!'

T'ta was all set to leave, royally ignoring us next door, when I deliberately accosted him. I bowed low over my greeting and forced him to acknowledge us even as he was in the act of putting the letter away safely in his pocket.

'Whose letter is it, Professor-saip?' I asked politely.

'God knows where you learnt your manners, Mr

15

Joshi,' he replied stiffly, 'but in Lahore we were taught that asking personal questions was a sure sign of bad manners.'

Then he turned away and left swiftly in the direction of the dense forest that lay at the edge of the village.

The junior clerk clapped a hand on my shoulder, 'There you are, maharaj,' he laughed openly. 'Witness now the departure of your hero into the dense forest to read his love letter in peace. Now he will go to the house of a woman called Kalawati. Arrey, I know all about the old rogue—for all his puritanical exterior, there is a Lothario lurking inside our crusty professor. Not for nothing has he left his wife in her village—he's never ever brought her here. Not even once!'

'Wonder how he produces so many children, though,' quipped Kheem Singh as he fried us a fresh batch of pakoras.

And we all guffawed.

'Have you ever noticed,' the junior clerk went on, 'how T'ta yells and curses us in Ingliss but coos like a pigeon to any woman he meets? And have you ever noticed how he behaves with that half-Chinese primary schoolteacher, Kalawati Yen?'

Ah! Kalawati Yen. I must tell you about her. You see, the British had once planted tea gardens around

Sunaulidhar and employed Chinese labourers to work on them. The gardens didn't take root but the Chinese did, and Kalawati belonged to one such family. She was an exotic beauty and in my opinion there was just one young man in the entire village who was capable of loving her as she deserved: me. So the thought of Professor T'ta trying to romance her had me in hysterics.

'Our T'ta is a real joker, I tell you,' offered the junior clerk. 'You won't find a character like him anywhere in the world, believe me. You have to write about him, Ma'at-saip!'

In those days, I was arrogant enough not to write on topics suggested by others, so I ignored his request. I wanted to write something that would be classical and modern at the same time, something that would blend D.H. Lawrence with Upton Sinclair, and Agyeya with Premchand. At that point, the character of Kalawati Yen and her Chinese ancestry appeared more promising to me than T'ta. Yet, while the pretext of researching her Chinese forefathers would give me a chance to come closer to her, it would also intensify my encounters with T'ta, her self-appointed guardian and bodyguard. How could I possibly waste my sophisticated intellectual aspirations on such a buffoon?

However, I soon began to see the potential of the

comic 'zero' in him because, despite being an international intellectual, I was also the local satirist and lampooner.

Professor Khashtivallabh Pant, Dubbul MA, 'T'ta' was a thin, short man, with a vanity that coloured every aspect of his personality: mind, heart and body. He held his frail body so erect that it seemed in imminent danger of toppling over any minute. He wore what he imagined was an Englishman's attire: a black-and-white pin-striped suit. This, however, only enhanced his comical appearance, especially as the seat of the trousers and the elbows of the jacket had patches of another fabric. Under the suit he wore a grubby white shirt with a limp tie hanging from a loose collar lined with dirt. Above it rose his withered neck which he tried to hide under a moth-eaten muffler. The crowning glory was a black Gandhi topi he wore to cover his thinning hair. Two features stood out in his cadaverous face: his sharp cheekbones and a Hitler-type moustache. His feet were clad in brown cloth shoes worn over white woollen socks full of holes. In my sophisticated city eyes, these pathetic hallmarks of poverty were terrific targets for lampooning.

Not only did T'ta admire the white man's attire, he was also deeply in awe of the white man's language. And so, he always carried a pocket notebook to jot down all those English words that he heard for the first time. This often led people to ask him the meanings of English words they knew he had never heard. However, T'ta acknowledged a word as new and acceptable only after he had consulted his dictionary, for he greatly admired the Anglo-Saxon mind for its quality of meticulous documentation. This is why he wanted all the 'junior log', namely, everyone in the village apart from the school's principal and manager, to address him as 'Sir'. He himself never forgot to affix a 'Mister' before he addressed any 'junior log'. As far as possible, he avoided greeting the locals with the usual 'namaskar', and preferred a 'good morning' or 'good evening' instead. If he was forced to say a namaskar to a local, as sometimes he was when confronted with a village elder, he added an elongated 'aa' to the word to make his greeting different from the rest.

Professor T'ta was genuinely proud of the fact that he stood apart from the villagers. His attempts to appear different from them, however, only succeeded in making him more comical. He mentioned Lahore in the lofty way that some people mention London or Paris, so that his three-year stint there accorded him a status in Sunaulidhar village that England-returned people are given elsewhere. In fact, he considered himself superior not merely to the villagers in Sunaulidhar but also to virtually all those who had never visited Lahore.

To some extent this was due to the fact that he was a brahmin in a village populated primarily by thakurs. Yet even among the brahmin families of the village, he believed his exposure to the reformist Arya Samaj in Lahore had given him an edge over the superstitious and ritual-bound Sunaulidhar brahmins. Indeed, he viewed them with such contempt that his son, Yatish, was forbidden to play with the other brahmin children in the village. And playing with the thakur children was, of course, out of the question, for T'ta had declared that he did not want his son to waste his time playing with children who were inferior, since he wanted to send him abroad. This is also why he was a stern teacher rather than a compassionate or affectionate father: his plans for his son had no place for compassion or love.

Professor T'ta struggled hard to escape the constricting village life of Sunaulidhar. When he first came to the school as a teacher, he had merely high school and Prabhakar degrees. To raise his own station in life and to lift the school to the level of a degree college at least, he was now a dubbul MA. His sights were set firmly on a college professor's job, so he never bothered to enrol for a schoolteacher's training class. He equated a lecturer's job with that of a professor and was somewhere secretly proud of the fact that, even if it was in jest, the villagers called him Professor.

The villagers, on their part, had evolved a cruel way of teasing this vanity. Whenever anyone from Sunaulidhar went to Almora or Nainital, he would bring back news that someone there had told him that T'ta had been chosen for a professor's job. Everyone would start to pester T'ta to host a party at Kheem Singh's tea shop and he would buy them a round of tea. For a few days after this, he'd appear less crotchety but as soon as it became clear that this was a false rumour and that someone else had pipped him to the post, he roundly cursed the man who had started the rumour and became even more cantankerous than ever. And then a fresh game would start in the school's staff room. How could so-and-so have done this, sir, they would tell him. You must do something about it; if you won't, shall we? Do you know what he says behind your back, sir? Shall we punch his teeth in? T'ta would rise in great agitation from his seat, let loose a volley of curses in English against the offender, bid everyone a curt 't'ta' and walk off in a huff.

T'ta's way of saying 'ta-ta' had its genesis in a faraway incident. In '42, during the Second World War, when he was leaving Lahore, regretfully, to return to his village after the death of his uncle, he encountered a few white soldiers at the railway station saying ta-ta to their departing mates. T'ta heard the word, asked someone the meaning, whipped out his pocket notebook and wrote it down. However, like most Paharis, he omitted to add the 'a' to the first 'ta'. Thus, for the rest of his life, he said t'ta instead of ta-ta.

Thanks to a stack of such notebooks, T'ta had a formidable collection of English words. He also kept a pocket edition of the Oxford Dictionary in his school locker and on the strength of both these 'weapons', he considered himself Sunaulidhar's greatest authority on the English language. This position was challenged by the arrival of Principal Shobhan Singh, who snatched away both the middle section English classes and the ninth class from T'ta's clutches. Principal-saip pointed out that Professor T'ta had no degree in English whereas he had studied English up to a BA. Moreover, he had been to good schools in Nainital and Bareilly and had a teacher's training certificate as well.

To demonstrate his contempt for Shobhan Singh's argument, T'ta started to tutor his son at home in English and sent word to all the guardians of the ninth-class students that if they wished their wards to pass the English exam that year, they could send them over to his house in the evenings. Offended, Principal-saip asked T'ta in the presence of Manager-saip, why are you teaching your son English privately, Professor saip?

Because I can, replied T'ta contemptuously, and because I am forced to.

Shobhan Singh said, if his teaching was good enough for the students of the schools in Bareilly and Nainital, how could it not be good enough for Sunaulidhar?

T'ta smirked as he replied that *he* had lived in Lahore and wanted to send his son to Oxford. What is your Nainital–Bareilly when compared to Lahore–Oxford, Shobhan Singh?

'You probably worked as someone's domestic help in Lahore,' Shobhan Singh countered, 'so don't tell me you studied there. And you may have passed some private exams by cramming rubbish from third-rate *kunji*s, but let us not forget that you haven't even seen the inside of a college. You are nothing but a village

23

bumpkin and I'll be surprised if your teaching will get your son admission even in Bareilly College. Oxford, huh!'

T'ta now produced a letter the principal had written, and pointed out several grammatical errors. 'Manager-saip,' he said, 'this school is as much mine as it is yours. My humble request, therefore, is to let English be taught here only by someone who has learnt it from an Englishman.'

'And which Englishman have you learnt your English from, may I ask?' spluttered Shobhan Singh. 'Just look at your pronunciation! You say "mayyar" for measure and "ood" for wood. Your English has all the flaws of the Punjabis along with the common mistakes that Kumaonis make. You say "bhast" for vast and "t'ta" for ta-ta.'

'Look, there is no point in arguing about this,' said T'ta as he left. 'All I know is that you are a mere BA and I am a dubbul MA. And I doubt if there is anyone in the world, apart from Manager-saip, who would consider a mere BA more educated than a dubbul MA.'

We will never know what Shobhan Singh would have said to this because often, under intense emotional pressure, his tongue twisted, and he began to stammer. It hovered now over the 'd' of 'dubbul' but got no

24

further. T'ta found his perfect exit line and left with an airy t'ta, convinced that not only was the principal incapable of arguing back, but that he was also reduced to a stammering idiot when faced with his superior mind.

The ongoing battle between the principal and T'ta over the English language became a source of entertainment not just in Sunaulidhar but in all the neighbouring villages as well. I found myself taking an equal interest in this verbal match and soon began to see the possibility of great comic characters in T'ta and the principal. The principal always wore the blazer of the Nainital school where he had once taught as a temporary teacher. He tried desperately to look and behave like the house master of a public school although he had probably never been inside one. Sadly, all he was able to achieve was a tight belt of disappointment over his sagging paunch and, of course, it did not help that audible farts often escaped from that tightly bound stomach. And then he stammered. Lastly, he was a verbose bore.

Now I had met several verbose bores before and

several people who stammered, but this was my first encounter with a verbose bore who also stammered. Moreover, he was a low coward who boasted about his brave Rajput ancestry. There was no politician, bureaucrat or intellectual whom he did not claim as his friend and if you named anyone of importance (real or made up), chances were he would claim to be best friends with him. He said he was an idealist and that is why he had chosen to come to a village, so that he could spread sweetness and light. Else, there were people in Nainital who were pressing him to become the principal of their school, he said.

However, Professor-saip had a different take on this. He claimed that Shobhan Singh had been chucked out of his job in Nainital because of his dreadful English. That and his bad digestion were his undoing, according to T'ta. Who could tolerate rotten English and smelly farts, he asked rhetorically. Would anyone in their right senses make an illiterate farter a school principal?

Not just the principal and T'ta, virtually all of Sunaulidhar was made for lampooning. I began to plan writing comic tales, like Steinbeck's *Pastures of Heaven*, and call the collection *Fools' Paradise*. The junior clerk was comic because although he claimed to be a poet, he had never heard of T.S. Eliot, or of that avant-garde poetry journal, *Taar Saptak*. He was a sentimental, lower-middle-class yokel who had the temerity to place himself alongside me—a progressive intellectual and vastly superior writer. He wrote third-rate sentimental love lyrics, generously peppered with archaic words like 'beloved' and 'ringlet'. Manager-saip, on the other hand, presented a Gandhian exterior, but was a secret tippler who lusted after one Mrs Nath, a teacher in the senior school. To me, Mrs Nath—a clever city slicker in the eyes of the villagers—was stupid because she preferred to flirt with the manager rather than with me, a sophisticated young man. Even Kalawati Yen, the heroine of my proposed magnum opus and several stories later shelved, even she was a comic character— Because she was preparing to pass her intermediate exam privately and, instead of coming to me, she preferred to go to T'ta for help.

In those days, any male whose aesthetic sensibility did not match my own was to me an object of ridicule. I respected all those who belonged to the lower classes: it was another matter that I had very little to do with them. Thus, in my callow youth, I could not see that I was as much a member of that Fools' Paradise as the others, and would remain a fool as long as I did not change.

At any rate, it was my constant endeavour to incite the mutual animosity between the principal and T'ta, so that the plot of *Fools' Paradise* could develop. I met them separately and convinced them individually that even I—who had studied under Lucknow University's legendary Professor Siddhant—had rarely met anyone with their command of English. Since, like the principal, I had been appointed by the manager, it was easy enough to convince him, but T'ta was far more suspicious of my flattery. Yet, this would call into question his own opinion of himself, so he finally succumbed as well. He accepted my suggestion that he should consult his Pocket Oxford Dictionary to select a really tough English word and then ask the principal its meaning when all the other staff members were present. And I told the principal that since he had mastered the complete works of Shakespeare, he should shame T'ta by asking him the meaning of a really knotty Shakespearean word. Before long, the staff room of the Sunaulidhar school became the site of an ongoing contest that began with both of them asking each other, 'Will you please explain this word?' The game became so widely known that soon a regular crowd collected outside the staff room to enjoy this battle of wits and I was elected its umpire.

The contest was evenly poised: despite his BA degree,

Principal-saip was unable to provide T'ta with a satisfactory meaning for 'northing', that T'ta had dug out of his dictionary, and T'ta was floored by the Shakespearean 'intenable'. I slyly suggested to T'ta that he introduce a new rule to the game: namely, that any word not listed in his dictionary would not be considered a valid word. Since T'ta was the sole owner of a dictionary in the entire region around Sunaulidhar, and since this pocket dictionary did not list many words that Shakespeare used, he had an unfair advantage over the poor principal.

This devious game took a strange turn when the principal pulled out 'logats' from *Hamlet* and tossed it at T'ta. When there is no such word, replied T'ta dismissively, then how can I tell you its meaning?

Are you telling me, then, continued the principal, that you know more English than Shakespeare? Look, here is the word.

T'ta promptly opened his pocket dictionary and said, go on find me this word here. I can't say whether I know more English than Shakespeare, he went on, but this I can tell you, maharaj, that I certainly know more English than *you*. Shakespeare may have used this word in his time, but today no one uses it any more; but what would you know about contemporary usage—you are out of date and bogis.

Anyone can tell from the way you speak English, the principal countered, that you have no idea of the language. What you call 'bogis' is actually pronounced 'bogus', maharaj. Your pronunciation is bogus, your English is bogus and your professorship is bogus as well.

Bogus, bogis, whatever, T'ta spat out as he rose to leave, you are a bogis principal, whether the word is bogus or bogis. A school up to the ninth and its head calls himself a principal? Has anyone ever heard of anything more bogis?

'*You* are bogus and bookish,' the principal said as he caught hold of T'ta's arm. 'Call yourself an authority on English, do you? All you have is a dictionary. Here, give it to me. Let me ask you the meaning of a few words—let's see how much you know.'

'Why?' replied T'ta. 'It's mine. And the fact that I have a dictionary and you don't should prove that I know more English than you will ever know. I read and write in it: if you had my love of English, you would have got yourself one by now, Shobhan Singh-jyu.'

At this juncture, the junior clerk could not resist adding that the dictionary that T'ta was so proud of was actually not his at all. It belonged to the school library and used to be kept there. Before he handed over charge to the principal, T'ta had slyly removed it from the library and hidden it in his locker.

T'ta looked sternly at the clerk and said in a trembling voice, 'I removed it from there because I had bought it with my money for the school, Mr Singh. I bought it when your uncle, the manager, refused to grant me the money to buy one. Of course, that he found the money to buy Mrs Nath her tablas and harmonium is another matter, but he could never find the money to buy the school a dictionary.'

On my advice, the principal and junior clerk prevailed upon the manager to issue orders to T'ta to restore the dictionary to the school library immediately, else a departmental enquiry would be instituted against him. T'ta produced the cash memo for the original purchase that he had carefully stored all these years to prove that he had indeed bought it with his own money, and that it did not belong to the school. He also produced the correspondence that he and the manager had exchanged years ago on the need to purchase a dictionary for the school and the manager's refusal on grounds of insufficiency of funds. Finally, he asked for the immediate dismissal of the junior clerk for making false allegations against him.

The manager was furious with his nephew the

junior clerk for placing him in this embarrassing situation. Don't forget, he told him sternly, that I can dismiss you as easily as I got you this job. Go, ask the professor's forgiveness and don't come back to me without his pardon. So the junior clerk apologized to T'ta who grudgingly forgave him. However, this episode left the junior clerk squirming and the principal seething at his defeat. The people of Sunaulidhar feared the dictionary as much as they feared God and, as its custodian, T'ta became a figure of reverence in the village. I suggested that the manager purchase the big Complete Oxford Dictionary for the school, but although he agreed to this in principle, he had recently blown the entire grant for the year in purchasing books on music for Mrs Nath and was unable to get the money together.

This is when the junior clerk suggested that we break open T'ta's locker and steal the dictionary. Go ahead, shrugged the manager, but keep me out of all this. My comic tale was now in danger of becoming a work of crime fiction and I can't say I relished the prospect. So one evening, I went across to T'ta's house when he was giving lessons in history to Kalawati Yen. Ignoring his cold look, I took him aside, put a friendly hand round his shoulders and advised him not to keep his dictionary in the school locker. How could one trust the likes of the junior clerk, I said. I wouldn't put it past people like him to steal it. T'ta shrugged off my hand rudely and although he told me, 'Mr Joshi, please do not disturb Miss Yen when she is studying,' he did take note of my warning.

So when the locker was broken, no dictionary was found and T'ta got another opportunity to write long complaints about his enemies. He had found the stub of a 'Berkley' cigarette near the scene of the crime and since this was the junior clerk's brand, he proved conclusively, with the watchman's testimony, that the act of vandalism was the work of none other than the junior clerk. Thus, another apology was notched to his score. From that day on, T'ta walked everywhere with the dictionary firmly clamped under his armpit and slept with it under his pillow. What is more, my warning convinced him that I was no longer to be classed along with the other enemies. At the same time, a seed of suspicion against me was planted in the principal's breast. To appease this, I pulled out a new novel from my trunk and extracted several new words for him to torture T'ta with, taking care to write their meanings in Hindi in the margin in case they were unknown to the principal as well. I suggested that he use the book to get by until the school acquired a better dictionary.

So the word game in the staff room started once again and T'ta found himself cornered with a fresh battery of unknown words. After a while he accused the principal of using words that couldn't be found in his dictionary, saying that he needed to see the book where they occurred before he accepted them as genuine. One day when the principal refused to give him the book, he snatched it from his hands and found my name on the flyleaf. What is worse, he discovered the Hindi meanings in the margins written in my hand.

So, T'ta smirked, his thin shoulders twitching in excitement, what kind of teacher of English do you call this man (here he cast a cruel look at the poor principal) that needs help in English from a *science* teacher? The principal wanted to counter this by saying, what about the help you take from your dictionary, but his tongue twisted around 'dic' and got no further. And T'ta waved his fingers in an airy t'ta at him and minced away triumphantly. I followed him out of the staff room, partly because I owed him an explanation but mainly because whenever T'ta left the staff room at that hour, he went straight to visit Kalawati Yen in the junior school.

That day, he was on his way there ostensibly to help her with some problem related to trigonometry. I followed him quietly and sat nearby. While T'ta was still studying the problem, I solved it quickly for Kalawati in her notebook. I then suggested that while she could consult T'ta on all other subjects—especially English, since he was the acknowledged master here—she should leave all her maths problems to me.

'What are you doing here, mister?' T'ta asked me sharply.

I told him humbly, I owe you an apology, sir, and have come to offer some help. T'ta relented somewhat at my humble tone. I took him aside and told him how the junior clerk had stolen the book from my trunk and given it to the principal. Don't worry, sir, I went on, I'll help you to forage some words from there that the principal just could not have heard of. One such word, I said, was 'hanky-panky'. I'll tell the principal to ask you its meaning and you say, 'hocus-pocus' in reply and walk out. This is what the word means but the principal doesn't know this and if he challenges you, just open your dictionary and show it to him.

So the next day, during the tea break in the staff room, Principal Shobhan Singh told T'ta, 'I was going to ask you not to do any hanky-panky, but how can I say it? You don't even know what the phrase means!'

As if on cue, T'ta muttered 'hocus-pocus' and left

the room. And when the junior clerk challenged him to give its meaning, T'ta opened his dictionary and said, 'I want to punch your face, but here it is: *yuch o si you yus, pee o si you yus*, hocus-pocus. There you are, maharaj, that is the meaning of hanky-panky.'

The principal was so enraged that he grabbed the dictionary from T'ta's hands and flung it out of the window. The dictionary hit a rocky outcrop and landed in the sewer that flowed out of the school toilets. T'ta's brahmin soul shuddered at such an insult to the dictionary. This was the last straw. He promptly sat down in protest, declaring that he who had thrown the dictionary into the sewer should now fish it out. But the principal wanted to wait for the school sweeper to do the job. To break the impasse and also to establish my secular credentials, I made a gallant dive and fished it out but T'ta refused to touch it.

'It is soaked in pee and shit,' he cried in horrified tones, 'it will have to be cleansed with Ganga *jal*—but since this will ruin the pages, the principal is welcome to keep it. Instead, I demand that the dictionary that has been ordered for the school be given to me!' he declared.

I ran to call the manager to resolve this fresh crisis and naturally, he made a mockery of T'ta's demand.

'How can something that was purchased for the school be given to a teacher?' he asked rhetorically.

'It's like that, is it?' T'ta yelled back. 'And yet your school manager can watch a teacher chuck a dictionary into goo and piss! When I was headmaster, I paid for that dictionary with my own money. I had bought it for the school and kept it right here, inside the school. If you give me one now, I will still keep it here in the school. I'll use it for the school,' T'ta went on passionately. 'But if you give that dictionary to this farting outsider, I warn you I will launch a satyagraha, because no one here seems to have any respect for Knowledge. This monster has just chucked The Dictionary into goo and piss! Well, what else does one expect of him?' he concluded smugly.

'Do you remember what happened the last time you launched a satyagraha, sir?' Manager-saip reminded him, smiling slyly. 'You had to run away to Lahore to launch your so-called satyagraha, Pant-ji. You couldn't even return to your own village after what you did there. You had to come to Sunaulidhar to seek refuge.'

'Then *you* had better remember, Manager-saip, that I am a Freedom Fighter,' declared T'ta in a voice trembling with emotion. 'Several eminent leaders know me from the time of the freedom struggle and it is because *I* spoke to them that your pathetic school was elevated to its present status. If I launch a satyagraha, they will have to give me charge of the entire school, forget a mere dictionary,' he went on. 'I will tell all the leaders of this country that the man you appointed as principal is bent upon dragging the school down into the stinking gutter that he tossed the dictionary in. I have nurtured this school with my blood and sweat and this is what he has turned it into! I had saved that dictionary for twenty long years and you have chucked it into a disgusting sewer. I refuse to remain silent after this, I am telling you all today. I will scream and tell the leaders the truth about this principal and this school!'

T'ta's voice became shriller and squeakier with each word and his eyes welled up. Finally, he burst into tears.

'It doesn't behove a teacher to cry,' said the manager in a weak voice, a little frightened at the spectacle of a weeping T'ta.

'And does it behove your principal to chuck Knowledge into goo and piss? I will cry, Manager-saip, so that I can purify the putrid atmosphere of your stinking school with my pure teardrops!' T'ta declared dramatically.

∾

Around this time, the principal spread a wicked rumour: that it was the professor himself who had dropped the dictionary into the stinking gutter. The junior clerk slyly added that the professor was so busy staring at Miss Yen that he tripped on a stone and lost his balance, and the dictionary went flying out of his hands and into the gutter.

I did not wait to see the purification of the school with the professor's tears because I was in a rush to reach Almora. T'ta had launched his teary satyagraha just before school closed on Saturday and, as Monday was a rare holiday, I did not wish to lose any time walking to Almora fifteen miles away.

I had barely crossed the Almora toll gate when a huge wave of laughter swelled inside me as the story of T'ta's absurd life began to tickle my insides. My friend Lalit lived midway between the toll gate and my house and despite how late it was, I went in search of him instead of first going home. I was almost doubling up with suppressed laughter as I called on him and even though his mother was waiting to serve him his dinner, I dragged Lalit outside. There, between uncontrollable spasms of laughter, I narrated the whole plot to him because it was so clear in my head. Titled 'Hocus-Pocus', my story would be about the supreme irony of the fact that five years after the English had departed from this country, there was a remote village in India where rival gangs were locked in a battle over the English language and a satyagraha was being launched to restore respect for an English dictionary!

We reached my place but my story was still incomplete. My mother was waiting inside with dinner for me but I just dumped my bag and we retraced our steps to Lalit's house so that I could finish telling him this great plot. We reached Lalit's and the end of the story was still nowhere in sight, so we retraced our steps back to my house. As we reached the deodar tree that stood midway between our houses, Lalit refused to go any further, so I stood there and continued talking and he continued to listen. We were oblivious to everything and only when Lalit's mother sent his younger brother to look for him did it strike us how late it was. Oh for those good old days, when cooking plots was far more important to us than cooking meals!

Over the next two days, Lalit and I continued to exchange ideas, and so many other stories began to emerge from the grand narrative of T'ta's life that I was amazed. There was the saga of the stammering farter, the principal, and the manager whose uncle had endowed the school with his no-good nephew; then there was the romantic poet of Sunaulidhar who considered himself the country's next Sumitranandan Pant; there were the hazy memories of the Burmese War tumbling in Kheem Singh's brain when it was fogged with the fumes of cannabis and, finally, there was the dumb blonde of the village—Kalawati Yen.

Lalit began to see a collection of Chekhovian short stories here but I had something different in mind. To me this bouquet was like John Steinbeck's *Pastures of Heaven*, stories about different characters whose lives were somehow intertwined with each other's. Lalit reluctantly agreed, but make Sunaulidhar a Fools' Paradise, yaar, he said. In those days, to people like Lalit and me, the world was peopled either with writers or with lumpens who existed only for us to write about them. Tragic tales were reserved for our own angst and those whose exploited lives we could only imagine.

I went to meet the junior clerk on my return to Sunaulidhar. I was told by him that T'ta was sitting in satyagraha in the manager's courtyard and that he had his son with him as well. He has written a long and furious letter of protest, I was informed, which he was threatening to send to the Education Department, the Education Minister and to all the national leaders he knew.

After I had related the plot of 'Hocus-Pocus' to Lalit and discussed it with him, I had promptly lost interest in it. I could not care less now about either its real-life drama or its fictionalized version. So I decided to express my passion for Truth by joining T'ta in his satyagraha, and told the junior clerk I wanted to put an end to this ridiculous farce. I had my own reason to protest and my satyagraha, I said to him loftily, was in support of the Truth. And the Truth was that the principal had thrown the dictionary out of the window and it had hit against a rock and landed in the gutter. I cannot support the lie that it had slipped from T'ta's hands after he supposedly tripped on a stone. He wasn't blind and he stumbled because, as always, his eyes were focussed on Kalawati Yen, a teacher in the primary section of the school.

I told the junior clerk all this loudly, within earshot of Kalawati Yen, and added that I would hold my satyagraha against all those lecherous men who stare at innocent and decent girls from respectable families. I also told him that if he did not retract his mischievous lie I would be forced to write about it to all my poet and writer friends. I hold the manager and the principal in great esteem, I said loudly with half an eye on Kalawati Yen, and hate to betray their trust in me. Go and fetch Manager-saip, I told the junior clerk finally, I have prepared a compromise formula that will appease everyone.

The manager arrived promptly. I took him aside and told him what this formula was: first, Principal-saip and the junior clerk must withdraw their false statements and admit that Principal-saip had chucked the dictionary into the stinking gutter. Then, I would tell T'ta that he would have to respect the principal's seniority because in the hierarchy of the school that is how it was. However, I would tell T'ta that he was more experienced and that henceforth the school would take full advantage of his superior experience.

The manager declared that he would immediately write a letter to his uncle, the generous Pan Singh-jyu, telling him that he should endow a library and call it Srimati Debki Debi Memorial Library, in memory of his late mother, and set a decent sum aside for the purchase of cupboards and books. The first book to be bought with this donation would be the latest and weightiest English dictionary. The principal and Professor-saip would be the joint custodians of this library and Professor-saip alone would be considered the librarian. The accounts of the library would be maintained by the junior clerk and he would be given an extra five rupees per month for his troubles. The old dictionary that had been fished out of the gutter would be placed in the library and the professor would be suitably compensated for it.

Everyone praised the manager for his compromise formula, but before Kalawati Yen could offer a glass of nimbu-pani with which T'ta was persuaded to break his fast, Manager-saip pulled out an orange from his jhola and stuffed it into T'ta's mouth. I almost succeeded in persuading Kalawati Yen to offer me the nimbu-pani instead, and I managed to hold her wrist for a brief, exciting moment.

To cut a long story short, everyone got something out of this deal: Professor T'ta the satisfaction of being designated the school librarian, the junior clerk managed five extra rupees every month, and as for the manager and the principal, they were secure in the knowledge that a cool sum from the promised donation for the Debki Debi Memorial Library would end up in their pockets. Lastly, Kalawati Yen was provided with an opportunity to come close to an intellectual like me.

∾

The junior clerk was after my life to write down my story about T'ta. Yet, no matter how hard I tried, I could never write 'Hocus-Pocus'. Once I have narrated a story to someone, I find it impossibly tedious to put it down on paper. In any case, I had another story in mind, in which I was the hero and the chosen heroine was Kalawati Yen.

Before accepting her into the story of my dreams, I got busy composing some verses for her—to get into the mood, as it were. But the problem was that no matter how hard I tried, I just could not get my pen to produce romantic lyrics. In these matters, I had always considered Lalit the more proficient genius, although as far as I knew, he had no love affair to inspire him. When I showed him my amateur verse, he suggested dryly that I write of Kalawati Yen in prose. You see, we were crass enough then to believe that one should write only after experiencing something first-hand. So I waited patiently for the magic to take place between Kalawati and me.

The trouble was that in order to come close to Kalawati Yen it was necessary to first get close to Professor T'ta. Eventually, he gave me the perfect opportunity, but in a manner in which he became the centre of my proposed Sunaulidhar idyll.

One Sunday, as I was reading *Jean-Christophe* and thinking of Miss Yen, who should walk in to put an end to my colourful fantasies but T'ta himself.

The minute he entered, he asked me sharply, 'What is this habit you have of lying down and reading, Mr Joshi?'

I got up hurriedly and mumbled, 'Welcome, sir.' I quickly put the novel on my desk and tried to straighten my bedclothes. I invited him to sit on the bed, and ordered some tea and pakoras for him. Then I drew up the only (and terribly rickety) chair in the room for myself. 'This is an unexpected pleasure, sir,' I told him.

'Your support for me during the sad episode of The Dictionary was an unexpected pleasure too,' he replied stiffly. He then picked up the novel I had put down, read its title 'Gene Kristoff' aloud, turned to me, squiggled his eyebrows and asked, 'Means?'

I resisted the temptation to correct his pronunciation, and explained that this was the name of its hero. He put the book down and fired a virtual barrage of questions at me: Why was a bright young man like me wasting his time reading novels? Why did I lie down and read? And why did I read a book in English wearing pyjamas?

'You must wear a coat-pant and a tie,' he declared, 'when you read English books; and sit properly at a

46

desk. After all, Sanskrit scholars have to wear a freshly washed dhoti and sit on a wooden *patla*, don't they? I can't understand,' he went on, 'how a high-caste brahmin like yourself can tolerate the company of the kshatriya manager and junior clerk,' he shook his head. 'People like them are up to hanky-panky all the time,' he went on. 'We, who understand the meaning of hanky-panky, must keep our distance from such riff-raff. And when there are so many brahmin homes for you to board at in the village, why must you live in a hovel run by that pot-smoking *halwai*, Kheem Singh? Do you want to ruin both your health and your wealth, Mr Joshi? I just don't understand,' T'ta continued, 'how you could have refused an offer to stay with me in my home.'

As far as I could recall, *he* had refused *me*! When I said as much, he brushed it aside as another instance of how his enemies were bent upon ruining me. What is more, he insisted that I pack my bags forthwith and go home with him right away.

I quickly calculated the pros and cons of this deal: on the one hand was the prospect of being bored to death but on the other was being able to sleep in a bed without being eaten alive each night by bedbugs. And, of course, there was the delicious possibility of meeting Kalawati Yen every day when she came for her lessons with T'ta. Once or twice, when I had managed to catch her alone and invited her to visit me, she had flatly refused to come to a public place like Kheem Singh's tea shop.

'Bhunderphul!' beamed T'ta when I gratefully accepted his generous offer. He added that he would charge me no rent but if I could help his son with maths and science, it would be nice. And I need pay him just two-thirds of whatever I was paying Kheem Singh for food every month, he added.

I had accepted T'ta's offer mainly for Kalawati Yen's sake. I had no idea that she was also the reason why he had made his offer in the first place. He wanted me to teach her maths, for—as I learnt later—he had plans to make her the senior maths teacher of the school. I soon realized that I had got a raw deal. For one, I was considered by the rest of the teachers to be a card-carrying member of T'ta's brahmin party in the school although I never wore a caste thread nor draped it like him over my ear when I went to pee. I thought I had already given proof of my liberal and subversive self

48

when I fished out the dictionary from the sewer. The other problem was that I was now forced to eat what T'ta considered wholesome food for the soul. *Khichri*, a gruel made of rice and lentils, was rated very high in his culinary preferences and his evening meal was a disgusting combination of rice, roti, lentils and some watery vegetables. Once a week, he would feed us sprouted beans and always served tea stewed with basil and pepper for good health. As a result, my bill at Kheem Singh's shop remained as high as ever. But the worst part of the deal was that everything I wrote had first to be presented to T'ta for a critical assessment.

Now, since T'ta's critical vocabulary stopped just short of calling Romanticism vulgar, my avant-garde stuff was beyond even being considered 'literature' in his eyes. Yet, there was no way in which I could tell him clearly that if you don't understand my work what is the point of my showing it to you?

His reply was, 'How will you know whether it is good or bad if someone does not read it first, Mr Joshi? Here, give it to me!'

This began to have a disastrous result on my literary output: T'ta would gleefully pick out grammatical inconsistencies and spelling mistakes. Mind you, I would have still put up with all this cheerfully if it had been

possible to get a few minutes alone with Kalawati Yen.
I was delighted when I first learnt from T'ta that I
would have to coach her in maths. Yet he would never
leave her alone with me for a minute. He had made it
abundantly clear from the first day that I was to teach
her along with his son, Yatish. When I protested feebly
that there was no point in teaching them together because
they were studying for different exams, he said I would
have to.

'Look, Mr Joshi,' he explained patiently. 'If you
teach these two separately, I will have to spend my
entire evening here. When will I cook dinner, tell me?
If they both sit together, I will save valuable time.'

I was astounded to learn that if I was going to spend
my time teaching these two pupils, it would save T'ta's
valuable time!

'I have to sit here,' he said clearly, 'to make sure
that there is no hanky-panky.'

'But why?' I asked plaintively.

He said mulishly, 'I just have to, Mr Joshi. Surely,'
he added darkly, 'you are not so innocent that you don't
understand why.'

'I can understand your concerns for Miss Yen,' I
replied, 'but can't you leave poor Yatish alone?'

And he said, 'I repeat once more, Mr Joshi, that
you are not so innocent that you don't understand.'

'But I don't,' I continued to argue.

So he shook his head in a resigned manner, as if he was explaining something fundamental. 'Do you agree that you are young?' he asked.

I nodded my head vigorously to say yes.

'Then, do you agree or not that this is a very dangerous stage in a man's life? That is why I have to protect Kalawati Yen, who is like my daughter. Her father is a hopeless alcoholic so she needs my protection, and Yatish I need to protect because he is my own son, Mr Joshi,' he finished.

The truth was that if he could, T'ta would not leave his son alone with anybody. Even when Yatish was sitting inside a classroom, T'ta would peep in from time to time to make sure he was all right. When T'ta was cooking in the kitchen, the poor boy was ordered to bring his homework there so that his father could see him do it. At night, he had to sleep next to his father and he was escorted to and from school by his father as well. The only time he allowed Yatish to move out of his sight was when the poor boy went to answer the call of nature. But even then, T'ta would pace outside the door of the toilet impatiently, and if Yatish spent more time than he should have according to T'ta, he would call out plaintively, 'Yatish, what are you doing there, Bhau?'

The boy got a brief respite from his father when Yatish's dinner was left for him in the kitchen and T'ta went on his evening constitutional. Sometimes, he would drop Yatish off at the village temple where a Bengali sanyasi lived, and ask him to teach his son some geography.

It didn't take me long to figure out why T'ta did not take Yatish on his evening walk. So it happened that because of T'ta's ever-present shadow over my life, I could only communicate with Kalawati either through sign language or by scribbling some messages on a slate as I taught her. Of course, these had to be erased immediately. In the beginning, these exchanges were really pathetic. I would ask a timid question to which she would answer in a flat, unemotional tone.

'I'm going to Almora. What shall I bring for you?'

'Haven't you heard, Ma'at-saip, "Ask and you won't get alms: don't seek, and you will get pearls. . ."?'

'What do you think of me?'

'Every man looks the same to me, Ma'at-saip.'

'You are very pretty.'

'Thank you.'

'I've written a poem on you.'

'How many others have you said this to, Ma'at-saip?'

Then, one day, she wrote something on the slate that lifted our lacklustre exchange to something different. She wrote, yesterday you won the hearts of all in Sunaulidhar, Ma'at-saip. She referred to a Pahari poem I had read out and a ghazal I had sung at a cultural programme organized by Mrs Nath the previous evening.

I promptly wrote back, Are you one of them? And her reply was typically cryptic: I am not different from the rest of the village, Ma'at-saip.

Emboldened by her slightly flirtatious tone, I scribbled, Why don't you come over here or meet me somewhere when Professor-saip goes for a long walk?

She quickly erased this message, shook her head vigorously and bit her tongue to suggest: Don't even think of that, *baap re*!

At this point, T'ta, who had gone for a pee, arrived and asked Kalawati sternly: 'Why did you bite your tongue just now?'

He looked at me sharply as he unwound the caste thread from his ear.

Kalawati said, 'I had made a mistake in the sum he gave me to solve, that's why.'

T'ta was not satisfied and picked up the slate to peer into it for the right answer. It had a solved sum on one side and 'Ma'at-saip', written by Kalawati, faintly visible on the other.

53

'This looks like a sum Ma'at-saip has solved,' he declared. 'So how was it your fault?'

It looked like an inquisition was about to start, so I quickly told him that she was dictating the answer to me and I was writing it down for her.

'Please don't do her this favour, I beg you,' he retorted sarcastically, and then sat down not in front but behind us.

Despite all this, I was determined that the next time T'ta set off for his evening walk, I would go to the cottage in the forest where Kalawati's father lived and start behaving in the manner befitting a lovelorn poet. In my mind I had created a scenario where the primeval beauty of the forest would descend through the spirit of the oak trees and fill my heart with music. I had already imagined the plot of a story where the poet/hero would meet the heroine. The hero runs to seek shelter from the rain under a tree. A clap of thunder draws his attention to the heroine, who is shivering nearby. The hero rushes with his umbrella and raincoat to her and covers her tenderly. He moves closer to her as she indicates that he should share the raincoat with her. A strange music brings them closer and the world of nature seems to conspire to make this union possible. Tragically, this drama set up by nature will end the minute the rain stops, and the two will part once again to go their separate ways, etc. etc.

But, alas, instead of bumping into Kalawati, I bumped into T'ta. We both asked each other simultaneously, 'What are you doing here?'

However, T'ta did not think it necessary to answer my question. He kept pressing me for an answer.

'I was just taking a walk, sir,' I told him.

He refused to believe this, for he said, 'I have never seen you take a walk before today, Mr Joshi.'

I put my meeting with T'ta that day down to coincidence and, three days later, went again in search of a romantic meeting with my heroine in the forest. This time I took a different route, one that skirted the back of her house. I hung about the back gate in the hope that I might catch her and call her over, when someone pressed my shoulder menacingly. I turned around to find T'ta glowering at me.

'What are you doing here, Mr Joshi?' he asked yet again.

I replied boldly, 'Bird-watching, sir. There is a pretty

little yellow bird that has been occasionally spotted in this area. Have you also come to see her?'

T'ta grabbed my arm roughly and dragged me away from Kalawati's house. Then he said, 'Mr Joshi, I don't come here to spot any bird, yellow or green. I come here to nab bird-hunters. This is the second time I have caught you here. And, despite your literary pretensions, the girl you refer to so crudely as "a pretty little yellow bird" comes from a respectable family. Her father is an alcoholic but her late mother used to call me *bhinju*, brother-in-law, because she and my wife came from the same village. So, in a sense, Kalawati is my sister-in-law's child, and I am a sort of guardian to her. Understand? Every evening, her father goes off to the hooch shop. That is why I come here, to be around, because the girl is all by herself in that cottage. And I'm warning you, Mr Joshi, that over my dead body will a Lothario like you mess around with an innocent girl like her. You aren't the first to have tried your luck with her, nor will you be the last. I warn you that while men like you may come and go, I will always remain her protector.'

'But I have no evil designs on her virtue, sir,' I assured him.

'Everyone says they don't, Mr Joshi. But youth is a

strange thing, and I can see that your eyes have been blinded by it,' he concluded gravely.

So this is how my story called 'A Paean to Nature' met an untimely death. I decided that I would stop hovering around Kalawati's house and, instead, started to write some terribly maudlin verse to woo her. There must have been something in it, however, because one day, as soon as T'ta looped his caste thread over his ear and went to pee, I hinted with a glance to Kalawati that I was going inside. She did not follow me. And when T'ta returned, he was furious that I had left my students alone. What is more, he saw something scribbled on the slate that had nothing to do with a lesson in maths.

T'ta let loose a torrent of questions after this: Why had I gone inside? What had I written on that slate before going in?

I told him I had gone in for a smoke and had written a theorem in Hindi. But he refused to believe me.

That evening, T'ta invited me to accompany him on his walk. We dropped Yatish at the Bengali sanyasi's and, as we moved on, he said, 'Mr Joshi, please do not leave Yatish alone like this with Kalawati ever again.'

I was stunned. 'Why, sir?' I asked.

'I have told you many times, Mr Joshi, that youth is a very bad thing,' he replied.

'But, sir,' I stammered, 'your son is hardly twelve or thirteen!'

'Some people mature early, Mr Joshi,' he replied darkly. 'Besides, Kalawati is not twelve or thirteen: she turned nineteen last month.'

'What has her age got to do with your son, sir?' I went on.

'Please remember that I have declared myself her guardian to make sure that nothing wrong ever happens between them,' he explained. 'My son is going through a dangerous phase in his life: an age when young men go astray, Mr Joshi, and I want to save his virtue in the same way that I want to protect hers. I consider this my moral duty,' he said and drew himself up importantly.

'But didn't you yourself tell me that her mother and your wife were related in some way? That makes the two of them cousins, doesn't it?' I persisted.

'I have told you countless times, Mr Joshi, that youth is a very bad thing,' T'ta repeated, 'and I may as well add that it often makes young people reckless and blind. In fact, in these matters even old people become blind.'

'Why do you say that, sir?' I asked innocently.

'Whatever I say I say from experience, Mr Joshi,' T'ta said solemnly.

'Does this mean that you have experienced certain base emotions from the time of your youth to now, sir?'

'No comments, Mr Joshi,' was the answer.

I decided to change tracks now. 'Sir, even if I believe that you became Miss Yen's self-appointed guardian to protect Yatish from her feminine wiles, what about all the other girls in Sunaulidhar? In fact, if I believe what you said about the effect of lust on old people, what about all the women in the village? Do you plan to become a guardian to all of them?'

'If there were any sexy sirens in the village, Mr Joshi, then would you come here for bird-watching, huh?' T'ta wiggled his eyebrows at me.

'But sir,' I persisted, 'didn't you say that even old age is not proof against sexual attraction? So, if Miss Yen is a sexy siren, shouldn't she also be protected against old men like yourself? You may look upon her as a sort of niece, but you yourself just said that lust can make anyone blind.'

I thought he would erupt angrily at this barb but he nodded slowly in agreement.

T'ta thought for a while and then replied, 'You're right, Mr Joshi. I am aware of this danger. That is why whenever she enters my house, I keep Yatish next to me like a shield. In the same way, I enter her house only

after her father, Peter, returns from his drinking binges.
Until that happens, I circle the house like a watchman,
and in order to make sure that I am never tempted to
cross the line of propriety, I have decided to take you
along with me on my evening walks. I think the greatest
danger to Miss Yen comes from you, Mr Joshi. So it is
best to keep an eye on you when I guard her.'

'And what if both of us get overcome by temptation?'
I asked him wickedly.

'Please don't talk such rot in my presence,
Mr Joshi,' T'ta said angrily. 'Sex may be a subject of
cheap jokes for you, but for me it is a very serious
matter.'

So that was how I started going for long evening walks
with T'ta. We kept an eye on each other as we guarded
Kalawati's house against other predators. Since this was
a chance to spot her or get a word with her, I decided
to ignore the misery of the exercise for that occasional
pleasure. Also, the plot of another story had started to
take shape in my mind now.

In my new story, T'ta was not the pathetic protector

of an English dictionary in a remote village in India but a middle-aged lecher who actually knew next to nothing of sexual matters. So now, my comic satire began to acquire the contours of an erotic romp as well. My hero was as ridiculous as he was lecherous and each time I thought of him, I would double up with silent laughter. I had never met anyone like T'ta, a man who could turn any topic into a sexual problem.

For instance, one day we were discussing Yatish's difficulty with maths. I said I found him a little weak in geometry. Suddenly, T'ta remembered that he had noticed Yatish carry his geometry textbook to the toilet the other day. Whereas initially he had been outraged at Yatish taking a book of knowledge into such an impure place, it struck him now that perhaps Yatish may be using diagrams from the geometry textbook to help him masturbate better.

When I gaped at his suggestion, T'ta said, 'I don't know how you can call yourself educated, Mr Joshi, if you can't see my point. Don't you know that our tantric traditions have always used the triangle as a sex symbol? Now if you tell me that this doesn't indicate some kind of sexual act, you will only strengthen my belief that you are actually a very ill-informed person!'

Poor T'ta was really desperate to keep his son pure

and good. His explanation was: 'Look, Mr Joshi, if a child gets distracted by "those kind of thoughts", then his interest in studies begins to waver. That is why, in ancient times, people would send their children to remote ashrams to study under a guru and make them take a vow of celibacy, Mr Joshi. Sex can really ruin a young man's body and mind, you know.'

Finally, one day, I asked him, 'Sir, did your mind and body get ruined when you were Yatish's age? Did you reach adolescence very early? Did you do something wrong when you were Yatish's age? If yes, then with whom, when, where and how? Please tell me all.'

T'ta's face turned bright red, and it was not—as far as I could tell—out of anger, but out of embarrassment. So I repeated my questions.

This time, he asked me two of his own: 'First tell me, Mr Joshi, whether you have crossed the line or not. If yes, then tell me, how old were you when it happened?'

I hung my head shamefully as I replied: 'Sir, I have to confess I am guilty. It happened eight years ago, and I am just twenty years old now. But I get the feeling that you were even younger than me when you went astray, am I right? I can bet you were even younger than your son when that happened.'

T'ta looked positively hunted when he faced me,

almost as if he had been caught stealing or something. Then he controlled himself and retorted, 'You have eight years' experience, you say? That means you were just twelve years old when you had your first sexual encounter! So I was correct in thinking that both Miss Yen and Yatish needed to be protected from you, Mr Joshi!'

'Whether you were correct or not, sir, the fact is that you seem a pretty colourful character yourself. Tell me truthfully, what were you up to when you were your son's age?'

'There is no point in harping on the past, Mr Joshi,' T'ta said primly. 'We should always look to the future. Yatish is my future and I don't want that he should get distracted by stupid things at this age. His whole future is at stake! I have had just one dream from the day that he was born: that one day I will send him abroad to study. He will get himself a degree from Oxford and then open a famous English-medium school in the hills.'

'And you will no doubt be its principal, sir?'

'I will be the manager of my son's school, Mr Joshi,' T'ta replied confidently. 'I will *appoint* principals. But all this will happen only if I can keep him on the path that I have chosen for him—and away from all tempters and temptresses!'

I assured T'ta that his son was pure as snow and that he was truly innocent where sexual matters were concerned.

'I can say this,' I told him, 'because once when some boy in his class had written an obscene word in his notebook, Yatish had come to me to ask what it could have meant. But please don't ask me to reveal what that boy had written, nor who had written it, nor how I explained it to Yatish,' I begged T'ta. 'I can assure you that your son is absolutely unspoilt, sir. Yet if you continue to dog his every step and police his every thought, you will rouse his curiosity. But if you ask me, I am more worried about you than I am about Yatish. You spend a longer time than him in the toilet, sir,' I added mischievously.

T'ta's face acquired that hunted look again but he pooh-poohed my concern by saying, 'I go to the toilet to empty my bowels, Mr Joshi. Perhaps people like you go there for something else,' he added slyly. 'I suffer from constipation,' he elaborated, 'and let me inform you that even Gandhi-ji took a very long time to empty his bowels,' he finished triumphantly.

'Do you also suffer from his compulsion to speak the truth and nothing else, sir?' I went on innocently. 'He has written about all his foibles most honestly: Gandhi-ji hides nothing about his life.'

'Mr Joshi,' T'ta drew himself up, 'I can assure you that I am as honest as Gandhi-ji. Like him, I have no problem in freely baring my thoughts about sex. Perhaps I should inform you that in these matters, I am a little more equipped than other men. In fact, unlike the puny youngsters that I see around me now, people like yourself, Mr Joshi,' he added, 'I am still pretty virile in these matters. However, like Gandhi-ji, I learnt early on to control my carnal desires. Otherwise, I can tell you, I could have fathered a child every year. But, as you probably know, I have just five children even though I have been married for many decades now.'

I found his argument a little specious. My face must have reflected my disbelief for he told me, 'This is why I don't discuss such matters with youngsters like you, Mr Joshi. You will be stunned if I tell you how I can control my orgasms so that I don't ejaculate if I don't wish to! As I told you, despite my virility, I have just five children.'

'Pardon my saying so, sir,' I said humbly, 'but couldn't this also mean that you have had sex just five times in your whole life? I find this argument can prove your weakness in sexual matters as easily as your virility.'

'Think whatever you wish to, Mr Joshi,' T'ta said loftily. 'Why should I waste my breath on people like you, who know next to nothing of these matters? Have you ever heard of birth control, Mr Joshi?'

∽

In those days, conversations about birth control were conducted sotto voce between friends, not like today when contraceptives are freely advertised on television. Anyway, I told T'ta that I had not just heard but even read about birth control.

T'ta was unimpressed and declared, 'The methods of birth control that I can tell you about, my dear ignoramus, are unknown to all but a few evolved souls like myself. In fact, I may be wrong but I think I was the inventor of these methods, Mr Joshi,' he concluded modestly.

'If you use these methods, sir,' I said, 'then how do I believe that other claim? That you could control ejaculation and all?'

'These methods are private intellectual property, Mr Joshi, I don't talk of them to anybody,' T'ta replied mysteriously.

Despite my many pleas, T'ta refused to say any more to enlighten me about his secret ways. His explanation was that he did not wish to let irresponsible youngsters like me in on such incendiary know-how and so become party to the ruin of Sunaulidhar's vestal virgins. God forbid, he shuddered, that he should commit such a crime against the innocent lasses of his own village.

When we returned from our walk that evening, I took out a book from my trunk and gave it to him saying, 'Read this and tell me if you find any of your secret knowledge mentioned here.'

The first question he fired after grabbing the book from my hands was: 'Are there other such books in that trunk of yours, Mr Joshi? If yes, then please make sure that the trunk is always locked. I see that you forget to do so. I don't want such muck to fall into Yatish's hands,' he said sternly.

And that is how Marie Stopes's classic text on birth control was handed over to T'ta along with a porn title called *Ideal Marriage*. He immediately covered them with newspaper and locked them in his cupboard. Occasionally, he was spotted reading them with the help of his faithful dictionary and would then tell me, I was right, wasn't I, Mr Joshi, to never leave you alone with Yatish and Miss Yen?

Professor T'ta first devoured *Ideal Marriage* during

the hour when I gave his son and Miss Yen their maths tuition. I noticed a certain flagging in his vigilant gaze and also that his trips to the loo were becoming rather frequent. But thanks to this, the minute I saw him loop his caste thread over his ear and hurry towards the loo, I would quickly scribble little billets-doux to Kalawati. It was in the course of our scribbles to each other that I discovered that T'ta planned to visit his village for Dussehra—so we would be able to get some time alone after all. I began planning what we would do and the two of us would giggle over the possibilities. So I informed T'ta that I had decided against going home for my vacations and would write my novel while he was away.

As if he guessed my true intentions, T'ta told me one day, 'You said that you wanted me to leave the house open for you while I am gone, Mr Joshi, but I have to ask you, why can't you write this novel, or whatever you were planning to write, in your own home in Almora? I must tell you that "the quiet" that you seek is going with me to my village as well. Her grandparents' village is close to my own, as I told you once, and I have already talked to her father about this. In fact, he is coming with us as well.'

So that is how we parted company: I left for my

home in Almora and T'ta, accompanied by Yatish, Kalawati Yen and her father, left for their villages. Ah, yes. Along with T'ta went my two books of erotica.

When Lalit heard my plans to write this comic-erotic romp, he said there was no point in going ahead with it until I managed to get T'ta to give some autobiographical details of his own past. That is where your title will come from, yaar, Lalit declared. And for God's sake, pay some attention to your heroine: How can you have a love story where the comedian is more important than the heroine? Are you writing a serious love story or the script of a Bombay film?

When I returned to Sunaulidhar after my vacation, a suitable title for my story seemed to be in sight. You see, the first day we went for a walk together, T'ta looked around furtively and then passed me a tightly rolled up piece of paper. 'Tell me the meaning of this phrase, Mr Joshi,' he said in a low voice, 'and then tear the note into tiny pieces, please.' The phrase T'ta had noted down was 'coitus interruptus'.

He watched me shred the note into tiny pieces and then looked at me for an answer.

'This means an incomplete sexual act, sir,' I told him. 'It is a birth control method as old as Adam.'

'Oh,' he replied pensively. 'I thought I had discovered this method. It is both easy and effective.'

'Oh no!' I said, 'it may be easy, but it is by no means foolproof, sir!'

T'ta looked rather disturbed at this, then recovered his composure and said, 'But I have always found it to be foolproof, Mr Joshi. This is what that book I borrowed from you also said. In fact,' he went on, 'I took this word down from there. I looked it up in my dictionary when I came here but, strangely, I couldn't find it there.'

'Read it carefully, sir,' I told him, 'the book also says that this is not a foolproof method of birth control.'

However, despite such private exchanges between us, I was no closer to getting any personal details out of him. I tried several methods: flattery was one. I'd pander to his vanity by referring to his virility but he refused to bite. All I got by way of a response from him was a mysterious half-smile with a twitch of his Hitler-like moustache.

'Men of action are not men of words, Mr Joshi,' he would say enigmatically. 'Those of us who have read The Book of Life,' he went on, 'have no need to read the books that you seem to need for knowledge. What can I possibly tell babes like you? Unlike you, Mr Joshi, I don't believe all I read. My motto is Do or Die!'

'So are you action oriented, sir?' I asked innocently.

'Means?' asked T'ta, a bit lost now. He fished out his pencil and notebook, carefully jotted the words 'action oriented', checked the spelling twice, and then put down the meanings I dictated. 'Thank you,' he said quickly, and stuffed the notebook and pencil away, saying, 'I have always believed that one should learn from all the people one meets. A true teacher remains a student all his life, you know. All these people who like to call themselves principals and so on, have all forgotten what they learnt, because they never kept up the habit of learning.'

'This means, sir,' I said in pursuit of my search, 'that you must have learnt something from Miss Yen as well, no?'

'Certainly, if she had anything to teach me, I would have, Mr Joshi,' he skirted my question neatly.

'But that is what I am asking you, sir,' I persisted. 'Does she have anything to teach you?'

'I am sure she does, Mr Joshi. The younger generation always has something that the older generation can learn. Look how I am learning from you!' he shot back.

I decided to change the subject.

'Sir, you've told me a number of times that Miss Yen is a siren. So what have you learnt from her about that?' I tossed at him.

'I have no desire to discuss such matters with idiots like you, Mr Joshi,' T'ta replied tartly.

'All right, sir,' I conceded, 'but at least tell me what you have told her about sex.'

'She is like a daughter to me, Mr Joshi!' T'ta was outraged at my audacity for even suggesting that he had any other relationship with her.

'Yes, but she isn't your daughter, is she, sir? And haven't you yourself told me that no relationship is sacred to a man made blind by lust?' I shot back.

'I have taught her nothing, nor learnt anything from her. And, if you don't mind, we will end this discussion right here, Mr Joshi,' he declared firmly.

So there I was being told one day that he had learnt a lot from me, and the next being told, what is there to discuss between us, Mr Joshi? You are such a child in these matters. What you have is mere bookish knowledge.

He was right in a way, but then I was so young that it was difficult for me to acknowledge the truth about myself. This is why one day I told him that in these matters, I was not entirely without experience.

72

'You've said this earlier as well, Mr Joshi,' he replied, 'but to date you have never told me anything that has strengthened my belief that you spoke the truth when you said so.'

So, one evening, while we were out on our customary stroll, I said to him, 'I am prepared to tell you of my past but on the condition that you will share yours with me, sir.'

T'ta quickly looked around to see if there were any eavesdroppers and then whispered, 'Not here, you fool!'

He dragged me through a thorny path that led us deep into the forest and then when the path dwindled and there was nothing but scrub and trees all around us, he paused.

I realized that we were standing on some kind of floor pocked with shallow scoops in the earth, almost as if it was the site of some secret ritual. God knows what the history of this spot was but I was pretty sure that it had some connection with T'ta's secret life because not only did he lead us to it unerringly, he even seemed to have some brooms made of twigs stashed away somewhere along with an old mat. He first swept the place, then spread the mat and gestured to me to sit. All the while, he held a finger to his lips to indicate that I was to keep silent. As I sat down, he cupped a hand over his ear to make sure that there was nothing around us, but all we could hear were some chirping crickets.

Only then did he say, 'All right, Mr Joshi, proceed with your story. Start from the very beginning and tell me everything: where it happened, with whom, and how. If you tell me all this honestly, then I will share my first sexual experience with you. So, where,' he asked rubbing his hands in anticipation, 'did you start?'

'I was twelve years old, sir,' I began softly, 'and lived then with my uncle.'

'You mean,' T'ta interrupted, 'that your uncle was the one?'

'What are you saying, sir?' I was aghast.

'It is what you are saying that is shocking, Mr Joshi,' T'ta replied. 'Tell me, was your first sexual encounter with a man or a woman?'

'A woman, sir.'

'Who? Mr Joshi, who was she? A relative? A maidservant? A neighbour? Or was it someone completely unknown?'

'She was a neighbour, sir.'

'But you told me the other day that you all lived in a bungalow and had no neighbours.'

I blanched. Quickly, I said, 'Sir, I was too embarrassed to say it was a relative, so I said she was a neighbour.'

'And how was she your relative, Mr Joshi?' my inquisitor asked next.

'Sir, I do not wish to elaborate on this relationship. That is why I didn't tell you that she was a relative.'

'One lie leads to another, Mr Joshi,' he warned me.

'It is not that, sir. It's just that sometimes it is embarrassing to tell the truth. That is why you keep silent, don't you?'

'Only if you open up, Mr Joshi, will I ever open my heart to you,' T'ta reminded me.

'I'm trying, sir,' I replied, 'but your interruptions make it difficult for me to continue.'

'But you don't tell me the entire truth, Mr Joshi,' he complained. 'Now tell me, how were you related to this woman?'

'She was sort of a cousin's wife, sir.'

'Sort of?' T'ta pounced on me again. 'What do you mean by "sort of"?'

'Well, she was my cousin's wife, so not terribly closely related, I mean.'

'Young or old?'

'Middle-aged,' I replied.

'Married, unmarried, or a widow?'

'Married.'

'Any children?'

'No sir,' I let my imagination fly. 'That is why her husband had remarried.'

'And did he have children with his second wife?'

'Yes sir. This woman was dying to become a mother. I think that is why she was attracted to me.'

'Hmmm,' said T'ta pensively. 'Perhaps she considered you a kind of child, then.'

'No sir,' I really pulled out all the stops now, 'I think she wanted to have a child by me.'

T'ta smiled pityingly at me. 'Mr Joshi,' he said, 'you can't even lie convincingly. If this woman really wanted a child that badly, then why would she choose a young boy like you, tell me? Why wouldn't she think of an older man to have an affair with? You said you were barely twelve then. Tell me, does any woman expect to be made pregnant by a twelve-year-old boy? Has that wretched Kheem Singh started you off on pot or something?'

'Oh that,' I brushed away airily. 'I said that to make an impression on you. Actually, I was fifteen years old then.'

'Look, Mr Joshi,' T'ta went on, 'if you trust me then tell me the truth. So, tell me, how did you know that this woman had designs on you?'

'Sir, she. . .' I hesitated.

'Go on, Mr Joshi. I promise you your confidences will remain safe with me,' T'ta encouraged.

Frankly, I had hesitated because talking of these matters in Hindi, except with a trusted mate my age, was impossible. So I resorted to speaking in English.

'Sir, she was an exhibitionist,' I blurted.

T'ta immediately pulled out his trusty notebook and wrote down the meaning after checking the spelling of the word. At first he could not follow what the word meant, so I tried miming it. When it finally dawned on him he bit his tongue, slapped his forehead, and his whole body seemed to get charged.

'Exhibi–' he tried the word a few times and finally gave up, then shot off a series of questions: 'When did she do it? What could you see when she did? Tell me all, Mr Joshi,' he was virtually panting by now.

Yet, as I spun my tale, he constantly interrupted me with questions: what sort of joint family set-up was this, Mr Joshi, that a woman could find the place and opportunity to exhibit herself to you?

So I quickly invented a daughter-in-law for this woman, a simple village girl who slept in the same room as her mother-in-law because her husband worked in another town.

T'ta was seriously puzzled by the complexity of the

plot now: how could she have a daughter-in-law when you said this woman had no children?

This was her nephew's wife, sir, I made up quickly.

'So all this exhibi– went on at night while this young girl was present?' he asked.

I had no other lie to offer except to nod my head. T'ta quickly drew a diagram on the floor. 'This is the room, right?' he asked me. 'This is where the exhibi–'s bed was, this is where her daughter-in-law slept, right? Let me get this straight,' he paused over his diagram thoughtfully.

'So, if this is the correct plan of the room,' he went on, 'then even if her daughter-in-law sat with a veil over her eyes, she must have been able to see something from the corner of her eyes, am I right, Mr Joshi? If yes, then she must have told someone in the house about these strange goings-on, no? At least her husband, Mr Joshi, don't you think? Such things can never remain hidden, Mr Joshi. I can bet that if what you have told me is true then this affair must have reached that exhibi– woman's *saut*. So your tale is bogis, Mr Joshi, totally bogis,' he proved jubilantly.

'You are right, sir,' I confessed, my eyes downcast. 'Our affair did become known. That is why her husband sent her packing to her father's house,' I was lying wildly by now.

'This means that you never reached the main point, Mr Joshi,' T'ta shook his head. 'That poor woman showed you all she had but you were unable to do anything about it!'

I bent my head in shame.

'Be that as it may, sir, this is all I have by way of experience. Now it's your turn,' and I turned to him eagerly.

'If you had really told me something worthwhile, maharaj, I may have,' T'ta replied smugly. 'But if all you told me is one big *gupp*, forget our deal. All I can say after hearing your story is that you don't know the first thing about a woman in love. Our women are action oriented, Mr Joshi,' he pronounced this new term proudly. 'If this woman and you had really had an affair, she would have devised some way of sending her daughter-in-law out of the room or at least found a suitable spot to make your "main point" happen. And if some woman had shown you all that you say you saw, then you would have been satisfied with nothing less than the main point, Mr Joshi,' T'ta proved his theorem with QED finality.

Since T'ta was adamant that he would reveal his secret past to me only if I told him mine, I tried several times to engage him in fanciful stories about my sexual romps. God knows how many trips we made to that deserted spot in the forest and how many stories I concocted. Yet all that T'ta would say to me is that you are a mere child in these matters—this is not the main point. And if you have never reached the main point, then spare me these childish fantasies.

He also objected to my speaking of my experiences in English. He had wasted so many pages of his precious notebook on new words that he was getting fed up now.

'What can I tell you when people like you, Mr Joshi, don't even know the Hindi words for the things and acts that I need to describe, *hain*?' he said one day. 'The truth is that you have done nothing! If you had, you would know the right Hindi words. For your information, Mr Joshi, our women talk in Hindi when they talk of sexual acts, not in English!'

So off I went one weekend to Lalit in Almora because it appeared to me that the comic character in my story was turning out to be not T'ta but Mr Joshi, the narrator. Lalit had just finished writing an allegorical romance where the poet was a cloud and his inamorata the thirsty earth, so there was nothing there that I could cannibalize for my own project. In any case, Lalit was as stupid about sexual matters as I was then. However, when he heard of T'ta's remark about women using

Hindi during sex, not English, he came up with a really far-fetched plot. 'Tell him,' Lalit suggested, 'that there was this foreigner called Isobel who had come to India to do a Ph.D on sexual symbolism and had appointed you as her Hindi instructor. Then he will believe that it was with her that you had reached the "main point" because you can tell T'ta that one evening after both of you were pretty smashed, she asked you what the Hindi word for the "main point" was.'

I agreed with Lalit that if I made Isobel a part of my fantasy, I could possibly convince T'ta. Also, Lalit had a porn novel called *Life of Isobel by Isobel*, and I could borrow many ideas and situations from there. And finally, I could tell T'ta that I can never use Hindi words to describe the sexual act because my entire sexual vocabulary was derived from whatever I did with Isobel and we spoke only in English. This would fix the old fox.

The more I thought about it, the more I warmed to Lalit's idea. I could tell T'ta that all you said was impossible was possible because it was all done with an Englishwoman and since you, maharaj, have never even come within sniffing distance of an English woman, what would a yokel like you know of these matters?

Lalit and I went from home to home and collected

a formidable collection of pornographic titles from friends: *Decameron, Adventures of a Casanova, Droll Stories* and *Fanny.* Some were borrowed, others were handed over by friends who enthusiastically supported my scheme. We'd all sit together and devise impossible situations and positions and my buddies would minutely study the tales and grill me so that I would be able to face T'ta's inquisition. If he said this was impossible, I was to say nothing is impossible with an Englishwoman, Mr Yokel!

Lalit was certain that after he heard of my adventures with Isobel, T'ta would reveal his past to me. We roared with laughter as we discussed the sexual postures I was going to describe to T'ta. Lalit also asked me whether progressive, left-leaning intellectuals like us should write pornography and I told him, well hadn't the venerable Hindi writer Yashpal written something similar? In fact, his critics had even said that it was pioneering stuff. So we agreed that as long as the aim was to expose obscurantism and humbug, writing explicitly about sex was not bad at all.

When I returned to Sunaulidhar, I spent many evenings among the ruins in the forest regaling T'ta about my sexual adventures with Isobel. This time, no matter how hard he tried, T'ta could not pick holes in my stories.

Finally, I turned to him and said, 'It is now your turn, sir. You have to prove to me that you were even younger than me when you did it, that you did it on a much larger scale and that even though you did it with a semi-literate or illiterate woman, she was in no way inferior to the memsahib I had fucked.'

The heroine of T'ta's tale was also a sister-in-law. And T'ta was merely three years old when his story began. His newly married sister-in-law was just eleven or twleve years older, and his story had its beginning in his ancestral village in his ancestral house that was known locally as the House of Widows. Some tragic strains began to enter T'ta's tale and I began to fear whether my comic satire was going to head in another direction.

T'ta was born into a family of orthodox brahmins whose sons had short lives while the daughters-in-law were cursed with living long. Their daughters were similarly blessed with long lives but the sons-in-law died young. This, T'ta deduced, was because the men of his family were sexually very active and that had a deleterious effect on their health. That is the reason why he did not keep his wife near him, he told me solemnly, because he did not want his own health to suffer.

Among the widows of his family was his father's widowed sister, Bubu, and the house that T'ta stayed in in Sunaulidhar actually belonged to her husband's family. T'ta's cousin, who was a little odd in the head, he said, believed that because he was called Shivshankar, he was an incarnation of Shiva. So one day, while in his Shiva avatar, he caught a cobra and wound it round his neck. The snake bit him and he died. T'ta's own father had died three months before T'ta came into the world, when his boat capsized during a pilgrimage to Benaras. And so T'ta became the sole male survivor in his family.

'The House of Widows'. I was enchanted by this title and another story began to take shape in my head. I saw a charming village home and on the second floor of this pretty wooden structure I imagined three little carved wooden window frames with a widow's face peeping out of each. Each sat silently at her window as she waited for a small child (little T'ta) to return from school. All day they sit there waiting for the child to come home and watch the world pass by. The central frame is T'ta's widowed aunt Bubu's perch, her narrow fair face with a long, prominent nose. T'ta's clan was famous for its long noses, that had given rise to the saying 'Their long noses are always up in the air.' Bubu's eyes are small and beady. She is the oldest of the widows in the house but the one with the most arresting personality. Even her widow's whites cannot conceal her regal bearing.

Bubu's eyes silently communicated to the villagers that even though her brother was no longer alive, they were never to forget that the House of Widows still had a guardian in her. So what if my younger brother died before his time, her gaze seemed to say, no one can touch a hair on your head as long as I am here. I am the oldest member of this house and now that all the men of my family are gone, I have come back to replace them. I am the one every villager comes to for advice and help. So if you once paid your land dues to my brothers, you will now pay them to me. I love this village more than my own life and perhaps the reason I was widowed so young and left childless was to ensure that I returned to this village to fulfil my destiny. If I had a child, would I have been able to leave my husband's home and come back to my father's? God gave me nothing in that house that would ever bind me to it. It isn't as if I don't have land and a life there: in fact, that village has a pleasanter climate and its lands are more fertile. Yet I chose this rough and hard village because I don't want that after all my brothers and father have gone, our household gods have no one left to honour them. I still go back once a year to my husband's home to collect my dues from the land there; but it is here, in my father's house, that I will spend the rest of my life.

The window on the right frames the sad, desiccated face of Ija, T'ta's mother. Her plain, dark face has a flat nose that does nothing to enhance her squat features, and her eyes have the pitiful expression of a spaniel. She seldom lifts them to look straight into the world, and when she does they are raised in supplication. She appears much older than her age, and manages to look destitute rather than poor. Her presence communicates one silent message constantly: Please pity me. There is so much that I want to do for you but I am a helpless widow. It was my fate that my husband died before me, perhaps my stars were responsible for the fact that we all lost such a fine young man. Where can I possibly go now? My father's home has neither the means nor room to give me shelter and my only brother has gone far away to Lahore. People say he has become a sort of sadhu. So I am fated to survive on the scraps my sister-in-law throws my way. The land we have is quite barren and even the rice we eat comes from Bubu's lands in the other village. So what can I possibly give you when I have virtually nothing myself, tell me?

The window on Bubu's left frames T'ta's pretty young cousin-in-law, Boju. Her rosy face has a dainty nose and two round eyes that struggle to contain their sparkle. Boju's rustic family had gifted her with an earthiness and a wide-open gaze that includes everyone in its warm sweep. Her merry eyes seem to accuse the villagers: How can you all have a good time when a young girl like me is being buried alive in this house of widows? All I have for company is Ija, that bovine aunt-in-law, who is so stupid that she cannot see that her sister-in-law has appropriated all the land and property that is actually hers by right, and allows herself to be bullied by her. On the other hand, there is that witch, Bubu, who will not let me alone for a moment. And just because I was widowed young, she forces me to live like a nun whereas the old hag flirts openly with men and has secret *khus-phus* conversations with them! She tricked my parents into accepting a proposal that she sent from her barmy nephew (my late husband). But why single her out? I accuse all of you for that deception—that is why I ask you now: Tell me, how do you think I am supposed to spend the rest of my life guarded by two jailors, in your desolate village surrounded by mountains on all sides? Tell me, aren't you all ashamed?

As soon as the child reached the chestnut tree at the corner of the lane that led to his house, three faces behind the window frames lit up. Bubu would order Ija to go get Bhau's tea and snacks ready and Boju was dispatched to get his face washed and clothes changed. Bubu would then step down to greet the child. She took his schoolbag and stowed it away in her cupboard and then while Ija and Boju got busy preparing for their tasks she would ask him to tell her all that had happened in school that day, praising or remonstrating him by turns. When he had washed his face and changed his clothes, he came to her and she'd hug him, kiss his forehead and tell him, 'Go, Bhau, go now to your mother and get something to eat.'

Bhau's mother asked him nothing. She listened to anything he said as respectfully as if he were an adult whom she could not interrupt or criticize. This child belonged to so many women that Ija had long ago accepted that she had no special rights over her own son. That right had long been appropriated by Bubu. Ija was shy to even show her affection for the boy. She felt guilty that she had deprived this child of a father because she believed that she was somewhere responsible for the evil stars that had ordained that he would die before his son was born. So Ija never ran a loving hand over T'ta's head or kissed his forehead. She had forgotten how to laugh or smile ages ago but she would not even weep in front of the little one. Yet once in a while, these frustrations frothed over.

This would generally happen when, after her customary screeching at Ija, Bubu took the little one to her room to tell him a bedtime story. When he started to yawn, Bubu'd kiss his forehead lovingly and tell him, 'Go, Bhau, go to your mother and sleep now.' T'ta would stumble sleepily towards his mother's room to find a moist-eyed Ija huddled behind the door of Bubu's room. Ija would pounce on the child, take him away to her room and lie next to him covering his face with her sari as her tears seeped through it and wet the child's face. The child waited for his mother to say something, to cuddle him, kiss him, but this never happened. She'd pat him softly to lull him to sleep and if he asked, 'What happened? Why were you crying just now?' 'Kay-ne', she'd say, patting him with each 'no-thing' she uttered.

Ija never opened her lips; Bubu would impale him with questions, yet T'ta gave guarded answers. The only person who spoke to him openly was Boju: she kissed him all over—on his eyes, his face, his lips even—unlike Bubu, who kissed him chastely on his forehead. Boju was just ten years older than him and she behaved with him as any loving sister-in-law would with her husband's younger brother, pulling his leg, poking fun at others.

Her full-throated laughter was the only sound of happiness he ever heard in this house of widows, so T'ta liked her best of all. Boju's husband was a dimwit who could never be expected to give a coherent answer, so Boju often forced her husband to call the little one over to their room and the three of them would play the kind of games that all young children play, such as *gitti*. T'ta's dimwit cousin, Daju, owned a chest where he stored odds and ends collected from all over. One of their favourite games was to pull out stuff from there and set up a 'shop'. The chest's treasures included his father's old badge, a Nepali cap, a khukhri, a broken mouth organ, an old and broken pocket watch, a necklace of rudraksha beads, a sliver of *shilajeet*, a stone with snake markings, a bunch of old keys, a blind papier mâché doll and a whistle that produced a croaky sound when you blew on it.

Unlike the others, Boju did not call T'ta 'bhau', or little one, but 'lala', young man. She would play pranks on both Daju and him. She often told Daju, I have to now act both the man and the woman in this house because my parents married me off to a halfwit. Sometimes, Daju smiled at her when she said this but sometimes, he would raise the khukhri and lunge angrily at her. Bubu and Bhau then had to wrestle with him until he calmed down. When T'ta asked her once, why does Daju get so angry when you say this to him, she smiled mysteriously and said, grow up a bit and I will tell you why. Then she kissed him, first on his cheeks and then on his lips. T'ta did not like it when she kissed his lips and scrubbed off the kiss with his sleeve. Boju went into peals of laughter when she saw him do this and often swooped down to kiss his lips again.

When he started school, she'd make her dimwit husband bring over T'ta's schoolbag to their room and rummage among the books. She traced words on a page with her finger and asked wonderingly, what does this say? When Daju was unable to answer her, T'ta said, *haw*, don't you know even this word? This is, *ka-ma-la*, *kamal*, lotus.

Boju draped her arm around Daju's shoulders to pull him closer to her, did you hear that, you fool, she would ask saucily. If Daju glared at being called a fool, she quickly added, I mean both of us, silly. The only one who is clever in this family is this little lala of mine. T'ta would be delighted to hear this praise but the next minute when she swooped down to kiss him on his lips, he felt angry and upset. If Daju frowned at this, she quickly planted a kiss on his lips as well. Daju was called Bholashankar—the innocent Shiva. And he was so innocent! Yet, when he had one of his spells, he imagined he was truly Shiva the Destroyer and threatened to burn Boju to a cinder with his third eye. Boju had to then worship his phallus to calm him down and Daju would smile mysteriously for a long while after this.

Boju was widowed just five years after she was married and Bubu declared that she held Boju morally responsible for her husband's death. Bubu said if Boju hadn't gone off to sleep that afternoon, Daju would never have slipped away, nor gone to the Shiva temple and wound that snake round his throat. Bubu refused Boju permission to return to her father's village and this is how Boju became the youngest widow in that House of Widows with T'ta as her only companion. He would steal Bubu's keys from their secret hiding place and smuggle tidbits for his friend Boju. Boju loved licking savoury, salty snacks. In fact, she loved to lick anything, and would offer a finger with some salty, tangy stuff for him to lick off. She often licked T'ta and—shame on her!—asked him to lick her back.

Boju continued to play gitti with her lala, and allowed him to take over Daju's treasure chest as well. The first thing that T'ta added to it was a glass marble he had found while digging in the field below the house. Then he added a bright crimson ribbon he once found lying on the way to school one day. Boju tied it on her plait and showed it off to T'ta. After this, he often brought back things that she could dress herself up with. Bubu always kept a strict eye on Boju's activities and whenever she felt the two of them had been talking or playing, she would drag T'ta away and order Boju to do some work instead.

It was different with Ija, though. T'ta and Boju needed to fear nothing when Ija was around and chattered away happily for hours. Boju was not the least bit afraid of Ija and told T'ta that his mother was as sweet-natured as a cow. Bubu, on the other hand, was a real witch, she declared. Whenever Bubu was not around, Boju would kiss him on the lips. When T'ta was about twelve or so, he started to threaten Boju that if she kissed him, he would report her to Bubu.

Boju folded her hands and begged him not to. She'll slaughter me if she finds out, she told T'ta. Since T'ta did not want his favourite companion to die, he never carried out his threat. Nevertheless, he did threaten Boju with Bubu's name to stop her from kissing him all the time. Eventually, she did cut down the kissing business, although she never stopped completely.

∽

I was deeply moved by this tale of an orphan boy growing up in a decaying house with three widows who vied with each other to smother him with their love. I listened entranced to story after story until T'ta started getting fed up with my unending thirst for an account of his childhood in that strange, male-less home. T'ta, who wanted to get to the main point, found these digressions very tiresome.

I, on the other hand, found myself hypnotized by the figure of T'ta the lonely orphan. The dirty-old-man character of my earlier story began to attract me less and less. One day, trilling '*Bhala thha kitna apna bachpan. . .* (Oh, the lovely days of my childhood. . .)' as I poured water over myself in the bathroom, I was stilled into silence as a picture suddenly flashed before my eyes: T'ta gazing up at the three windows to find his favourite childhood companion dressed in white widow's weeds, her laughing eyes dull. This is why, when T'ta started using the crude gutter language of a pornographic novel to describe his sexual adventures with Boju, I felt nauseated. The House of Widows and the pathos of its lonely lives were destroyed forever.

Meanwhile, T'ta's story continued to move inexorably towards its main point. It so happened that the day T'ta came home after his last school-leaving exam, the three widows greeted him with fresh enthusiasm.

'This is the end of your studies,' Bubu declared in a satisfied tone. 'Now you will take charge of this house and look after us, Bhau!'

But her bhau had other plans: He refused to spend the rest of his life in this suffocating atmosphere and told Bubu that he wanted to go away to study further.

'Go where?' Bubu asked.

'To Lahore,' replied T'ta confidently. 'Send me to my uncle there.'

Bubu promptly refused to give her permission. This was the first time that she had refused him anything and T'ta was both furious and hurt. He confided his feelings to Boju because he had seen how often Bubu had behaved similarly with her.

Boju gazed lovingly at her lala's brimming eyes and pulled him to her breast.

'Now you are all grown up, aren't you?' she asked him lovingly. 'Then why are you afraid of that old witch? You know how to read and write. If you want to go to Lahore so badly, why don't you write your uncle a letter? All you need is a postcard and I have an old one lying around somewhere.'

So Lala wrote to his uncle in Lahore on the postcard

Boju fished out for him. T'ta's uncle worked as a proofreader in a newspaper office in Lahore. He had become an Arya Samaji and was respected as a holy man there. Defying Bubu, on Boju's instigation, also gave T'ta the feeling that he was no longer a child to be told what he could and could not do. He was now a grown-up man. He had already got proof of this fact when he had smelt something heady in the spices and sweat that emanated from between Boju's breasts. After all, don't forget, his family's famous long nose was renowned for its superior smelling skills as much as it was celebrated for its pristine brahmin lineage.

Boju's eyes welled up with tears when she heard that he had sent off the letter. 'You were my only supporter in this house of widows, lala. If you go away, how will I pass my days?' she asked him sadly.

So he hugged her and replied, 'I'll call you over, too. I promise. I'm a grown-up now, I'm not afraid of anyone.'

Boju smiled as she wiped her eyes. 'What on earth will I do in Lahore, lala?'

And her newly grown-up lala answered confidently, 'You can also start studying. Then you will be able to get a job and become independent.'

'Will I be able to marry again?' she asked him saucily.

'Why not?' answered her self-assured new lala. 'The Arya Samajis there are progressive social reformers and they promote widow remarriage.'

'Who will I marry, then? Your uncle?'

'No, you can't do that because my uncle is a confirmed bachelor,' Lala replied solemnly. 'He's taken a vow of celibacy.'

Boju pulled him close to her and rolled her eyes, 'So then who will I marry? You? Answer me, Lala.'

Lala was stunned. Then he shyly shook his head to refuse her proposal.

Boju laughed ecstatically at his obvious discomfiture.

'Who would marry you anyway, Lala?' she asked him. 'You still wipe your lips with your sleeve if a woman kisses you. Forget it! You are still such a baby. Tell you what,' she went on, 'I'll come to your Lahore, lala, but not to study. I'll watch how you study, look after you, do whatever you ask me to do, all right?'

After this, she swooped and kissed him on the lips—something she rarely did now. But with this kiss, Lala realized that he was now a man, no longer the child he was before. For the first time, he did not feel the need to scrub his lips or push Boju away. Also, he realized that Boju's kiss this time was not like the other pecks she had teased him with earlier. This one was a grown-up kiss that went on and on, her lips firmly glued to his. He found the sensation so pleasing that he wondered why he had stopped her earlier. His breath came in quick gasps when she finally let go and his gaze was instinctively drawn to her rapidly rising and falling bosom. Boju noticed the way his gaze lingered on her breasts and asked him slyly, 'Want to suckle, Lala?'

She had barely unbuttoned her blouse and bared her breasts when they heard Bubu's footsteps, and Boju scooted away. Khashti was furious and his mind tried to figure out a way in which he could get rid of Bubu so that he could complete his unfinished business with Boju.

A few days after this episode, Bubu decided it was time she visited her lands in the other village. Every year, when she went to her husband's village, Bubu took Boju with her as a companion and helping hand. This time, however, because Ija was not well, she was forced to go alone. But before she departed, she left strict instructions that Boju was to sleep in Ija's room at night and look after the kitchen and house in her absence. Of course this meant nothing to Boju, for dealing with the simple Ija was a breeze compared to dodging the eagle-eyed Bubu. She became so bold that sometimes she surprised herself with her daring and managed to do so much with Lala even while Ija was sleeping in the same room, that he almost choked with fright sometimes.

Three days after Bubu left, Lala's uncle replied, inviting him warmly to stay with him in Lahore. The whole day Lala and Boju discussed the offer and both felt deeply sad at the prospect of Lala's imminent departure.

And that night, their affair reached its Main Point.

It all happened in the cramped attic that had curious angles and corners, which you only reached after climbing the stairs from Ija's room and going past the prayer room. That night, as soon as Ija dozed off, Boju signalled Lala to follow her. They crept upstairs to the crooked attic, once the family's bustling kitchen. Now, it was an abandoned dump with old pots and pans and rubbish lying everywhere. Moonlight streamed through the slits where the old slate tiles of the roof had shifted, and Boju had to stuff her pallu in her mouth to stop her screams of delight when she came.

This was also when T'ta learnt that his widowed Boju was a virgin.

The next day she asked him, 'Why did you do all that with me if you don't want to marry me? After what happened between us last night, I'm not going to let you leave me alone here and go off to Lahore, Lala.'

When he promised her he would take her with him she laughed, 'Tell your Bubu that and see what happens. I'm sure she'll break both your legs and my head as well. Suppose she doesn't allow us to go, then what will you do? Tell me.'

'Then I won't go either,' he told her shyly. 'I can't live without you now.'

Disregarding Ija's presence in the nearby kitchen, Boju took him into her arms and said, 'If this is how you feel, then why go at all? Tell Bubu that you wrote to your uncle because I had instigated you to.'

'But won't she be furious with you if I say that to her?' he asked her weakly.

'When has that hag ever been happy with me?' Boju shrugged. 'But, you idiot, have you ever thought what she is going to think of us if you did say that?'

Two weeks later, Bubu returned from Sunaulidhar. As soon as she heard about his uncle's invitation, she declared firmly that T'ta could not go. He was needed here; this house needs a man, she told him. And I don't think that your writing to him without first taking my permission was a good thing, Bhau, she told him through pursed lips. This was the first time he had been ticked off by Bubu, but what hurt him more was her anger at Boju's role in the episode. Moreover, Bubu's famous nose (that could smell anything rotten, from odours to underhand deals) started to twitch ominously. And after this she made sure that Lala and Boju were never left alone together. Boju took this as a challenge to become even more daring and reckless.

There was just one time in the entire day when Bubu took time off from policing the two. Each morning, she went to the prayer room to bathe her gods and say her prayers. As soon as they heard the sound of the tinkling bell that signalled that the rituals were over and she would now pick up her prayer beads to meditate, they knew that nothing would make her leave her seat for the next half hour or so. The opening and closing chants of the prayer were recited loudly and it took her about twenty minutes between the two. Boju had calculated that this was the best time, because Ija would be downstairs in the kitchen brewing tea to serve Bubu immediately after her puja. And even if Ija comes in, she told him boldly, I know she'll still believe your innocence, not what her eyes see, Lala.

He accepted Boju's fearless plans with a trembling

heart and made love to her while Bubu was busy bathing her gods upstairs. Gradually, he was lulled into believing that even if—unlikely, but even if such a thing happened—Bubu decided to step downstairs, Boju's sharp eyes and ears would know and Bubu would never discover what they were up to.

Then one day, the impossible happened. So engrossed were the two of them in each other's bodies that they did not hear Bubu's closing mantra that signalled her return, and Bubu saw it all. She saw it but kept quiet.

'Perhaps she never saw anything,' Boju told the terrified Lala. 'Do you think the old hag would remain quiet if she had?'

How wrong she was.

That very day, Bubu sent for her trusted companion who had escorted her to Sunaulidhar. Then she packed Bhau's clothes and bedding with her companion's help, ran a loving hand over the lala's head and said: 'I don't want you to give up the chance of a lifetime, Bhau. You are right: if you stay in this village any longer, you will ruin your future. Remember your father was a learned man too. So go to Lahore and stay with your uncle and come back a learned man as well.'

Khashti said nothing. He realized then that Bubu

knew. He wished he could tell her that he did not want to leave Boju, but he could not find the courage to open his mouth. Nor could he dare to say a private goodbye to Boju for she was nowhere to be found. He peeped into Ija's room, the puja room, the kitchen—but Boju had simply disappeared. Then he heard the sound of someone sobbing in Bubu's room and hurried towards it.

The room was padlocked.

He debated whether to knock on the door, but before he could decide, Bubu arrived.

'What are you looking for?' she asked him sternly.

'Boju?' he asked in a low voice.

'Your Boju has been sent to her parents' home, bhau. The poor thing hadn't visited her parents for so long. I thought it might take her mind off from things here,' Bubu replied blandly.

'When did she leave?' he asked in a hoarse voice. 'With whom?'

'When you were bathing, Bhau,' she replied. 'Now hurry up and leave, otherwise it will be dark before you reach Almora.'

∾

After he reached Lahore, T'ta could never muster up the courage to ask about Boju in the letters he wrote home and, of course, Bubu never mentioned her in her letters to him either. Bhau took this to mean that Boju was still with her parents and once when he finally wrote her a letter, knowing full well that she could neither read nor write, he never got a reply.

His uncle died almost as soon as he reached Lahore and a stunned Bhau was sent off to one of his colleagues, also an Arya Samaji and missionary like his late uncle. In return for the favour of being allowed to study while staying at this man's house, Bhau had to clean and cook for his host. He often thought of Boju and imagined her in her pretty village. She had told him many stories about it: how the sun's rays winked on the mica chips in the dust, how the pure gurgling springs became waterfalls as they gushed over the steep hillsides and how, occasionally, big boulders tumbled down to fall with a splash into the raging torrent in the valley far below. Often, someone leapt to death into the river and she would mimic the sound of the falling person's scream as they heard it in the village, piercing the silent night.

In fact, the two of them played a game where he became the river in the valley and lay on the floor and she crouched on the bed over him and pretended to be the mountain that towered over it. She would stand over him, wave her hand to indicate a falling boulder and then with a loud 'gud-gud-gud' sound, would lose it in Lala's body, the 'river'. Both of them giggled as they made the splashing and sucking sounds the boulder made as it sank to the bottom of the river.

Years later, he found out what happened to his Boju after she left for her parents' village with Bubu's trusted companion, Kisaniya the blacksmith. He heard the story from Boju's childhood friend Piruli, who told him that Boju had never reached the village because she met with an accident on the way. On one of the several hairpin bends, a huge boulder fell on her and pushed her over the edge and into the river below. They never found her after that, Piruli said. The last person to see her alive was Kisaniya the blacksmith, Bubu's escort.

I tried several times to write a story called 'The House of Widows' but something always held me back. The image of the three widows framed in the windows disturbed me deeply. I wanted to write something tragic, with an underlying note of such sadness that it would haunt the reader all his life. Yet, every time I tried to write of T'ta's innocent seduction and coming of age, the lecherous old man that he had now become intruded rudely. I began to feel like a voyeur, and was aware that even if it was in the cause of literature, I was committing a hideous sin by trivializing the tragedy of that childhood romance. I just couldn't do it. I just could not get my pen to marry the comic with the pornographic, that innocent first love with an old man's lust, and introduce sex and violence into a rural idyll. Try as I might, I could never find an adequate plot to convey the many layers of T'ta's childhood in the House of Widows.

On my next trip to Almora, when I narrated a tentative plot to Lalit, studded with adjectives such as 'tragic', 'hesitant', 'unspoken', he wasn't particularly moved. I had to regretfully agree with him that while the comic-erotic T'ta story had the potential of a biting satire, the gothic tale of the widows was strictly for decadent romantics, not for progressive writers like us.

'The comic will work, comrade,' he told me finally, 'but not the pathetic.'

I decided that I should leave 'The House of Widows' alone for the present and try something that would give me the courage to attempt it again. So I wrote a story called 'The Chowkidar's Son' to test the waters with my literary community. Lalit agreed that this was the best strategy. The famous leftist critic Dr P.C. Gupta was visiting Almora then and a literary gathering had been organized in his honour by the lawyer Harishchandra Joshi at his house the following Friday. Lalit told me to immediately churn out my story and have it ready by then. If P.C. Gupta passes it, he said, then no one would dare to criticize it. I got down to the task right away. The story was about the young son of an old watchman, bullied both by his father's new wife and the mistress of the house. After his opium-addict father dies, he begs the owner to appoint him in his father's place. Then, he waves the bunch of keys in his stepmother's face to let her know that he has taken his father's place in every sense of the word.

Despite the proletarian origins of the hero and despite all the heavy-with-an-unutterable-sadness kind of language, P.C. Gupta did not like it one bit. He ticked me off sharply for writing on the 'lumpen proletariat' and said I should leave such plots for pulp writers: he expected better work from an intelligent and progressive writer of my generation.

Smarting from this public humiliation, I tore the manuscript into shreds and chucked it away angrily as

I walked home after the meeting, flinging it in the direction of the town's old cremation grounds. Lalit and I were so young and dramatic then that such gestures meant a lot to us. In fact, words, ideas and gestures meant so much to us that we became characters not individuals. We saw ourselves as fiery revolutionaries who would usher in the brave new world that was waiting to be born.

So 'The House of Widows' was shelved and whatever I heard from T'ta on our walks pushed it further into the background. Since I had backed T'ta in his feud with the school manager and since the feud was acquiring political overtones, our conversations during the walk turned to politics. T'ta also believed that my interest in his life's story was a ruse to seek his permission for a Main Point kind of encounter with Kalawati Yen. So he made sure that I did not come within even sniffing distance of her and, forget the main point, he was determined that I did not even make it past the first point.

My interest in T'ta's story flagged as I became aware that my own story had not progressed at all.

108

T'ta's heavy policing would not let us do anything more than exchange a few sentences on the slate but here at least there was some cause for cheer as I began to sense that she was warming to me. I had passed on some of Lalit's verse and she was deeply moved for I saw her blush. So when I scribbled: I have written romantic poetry for you but you haven't replied even in prose, she quickly scribbled some lines from a film song: '*Dum bhar jo udhar munh phere, O chanda, main tujhse pyaar kar loongi, baatein hazaar kar loongi.*..(If only the moon would look the other way for a moment, I would make love to you, say a thousand things to you...)'

I was delighted, but the *chanda* she referred to refused to look the other way. I decided then that, like T'ta's Boju, I would dive into dangerous action and that is how I succeeded in some necking and petting. T'ta could not escort Kalawati home because the junior school, where she taught, gave over before T'ta's senior school. So I took to walking her home after giving my class some writing work to do in my absence. I'd wait for her at an old haunted hut on the way and we would walk together. So 'The House of Widows' no longer remained a tragic tale but became, instead, a story of lust and longing.

And then, one day, we were caught. Not in the

haunted hut but in T'ta's house. T'ta said nothing then but his determination to put a firm end to this budding relationship was no less than Bubu's had been when she drove Lala and Boju apart. Kalawati's exams were drawing near and she had to go to Nainital to take them. T'ta took Yatish and her away and on his return thanked me on her behalf, adding that as Miss Yen no longer had need of my help, I should not try and meet her again.

Stung, I told him that my feelings for her were always pure; the only interest I had in her was the kind that a caring teacher has for his student. We never wrote anything on that slate that was not connected with maths and if you are referring to my holding her hand that day, I have an explanation for that as well, sir, I said. The poor thing was not feeling well and I was taking her pulse.

I have felt the pulse of the times, Mr Joshi, replied T'ta. Tell me, are you willing to make an honest woman of her? Do you have the guts to tell your brahmin family that you are involved with a Christian half-caste? If not, then stop feeling her pulse and stay away from her. Tell me, will you marry her? Shall I approach your family with this proposal? Shall I?

Like most brave revolutionaries, I was actually a

low coward. So I could not tell him that I want to make her mine and have no fear in confronting my family with this fact. Instead, I repeated that my intentions were honourable and that she meant no more to me than any other student. You, not I, have dirty thoughts about her, I told him. I know what you wrote on that slate, Mr Joshi, T'ta threw back at me, and I know what it means. What, I asked him. He quickly put a finger to his lips and indicated that this was not the place to discuss that.

He dragged me to our secret place in the forest and the story he told me there turned my stomach. It was something straight out of a soft-porn magazine and put paid to any intentions I may have had of writing a proletarian love story. Although other well-known writers were doing such stuff, I couldn't get myself to attempt something that would not be acceptable to P.C. Gupta and betray the grand narrative tradition of the great Premchand.

The essence of T'ta's new story was this: a furtive love affair conducted in a lower-middle-class family. Its hero was T'ta and the heroine a girl who, despite being named Prempyari (the beloved), was neither lovely nor loved. Nor could she, despite her name, evoke romance in any person except in someone like T'ta.

When T'ta moved to his uncle's friend's house in Lahore to complete his studies, he met a girl there who was a distant niece of the man. She was about four or five years older than T'ta and helped her aunt with the housework and children while studying for her matric exam in Punjabi. So both T'ta and she were the unpaid household helpers who were actually students earning their keep. Their common predicament was what first drew them close to each other. He was good at his studies, she was hopeless. So she sought his help. On the other hand, our hero—brought up as the only male child in the House of Widows—did not even know how to sew a button on to his shirt. So he needed her help as well. The matter first started with her coming to him for help with her maths homework, and the slate became their medium of exchanging life stories with each other.

Like the hero's crush on his pretty Boju, the heroine too had one on her brother-in-law, whom she called Jijja. This man was married to a distant cousin, a venomous shrew called Vadde Bhenji ('elder sister' in Punjabi). Vadde Bhenji was suspicious of the heroine's every move and was just the kind of figure in her life that Bubu was in the hero's.

'I was just nine years old when I was orphaned,' the heroine told our hero, 'when Vadde Bhenji took me to live with her.'

'I was orphaned before I was born,' he replied.

'Oh you poor thing!' she said. 'So I was brought up by them,' she went on, 'doing all I could to help them run their home and look after their children. Vadde Bhenji lolled on her bed all day leaving all the housework to me. But when I turned twelve, her ears pricked up each time Jijja-ji spoke to me lovingly. One day, he bought me a 14-carat gold chain and she caught him putting it around my neck. She was livid, and threw me out of her house. That is why poor Jijja-ji sent a frantic telegram to his relative, bought me a ticket for Lahore and sent me to this house. I was fifteen then and it has been a full five years since that day. These people are so happy to get a free maid that they never even think of getting me married or anything!'

Since the heroine was an orphan, she adopted our hero as a *rakhi* brother. Once this relationship was established, no one had any serious objection to her going into his room to study after she completed her chores at night. When she tied the sacred thread on his wrist, she had said to him rather dramatically, 'I have no protector but you in this whole wide world. Promise me, you will always stand by me no matter what happens.'

The hero promised her his undying protection. As

113

long as they hid the real nature of their relationships with Boju and Jijja from each other, nothing came in the way of their maintaining a safe, uncomplicated affection. In any case, she was so unattractive, her voice so harsh and, in general, she was so crude and fat that there was little chance of any sexual attraction developing between the two.

Then, slowly, almost insidiously, she began to ask the hero about Boju. At first he was a little hesitant and wondered whether a brother and sister ought to exchange such information. When she pooh-poohed these doubts away, he innocently told her all about his affair with Boju. Having got that off his chest, he asked her about her Jijja.

At first, she swore that her relationship with him was not 'like that'. The hero was angry at her betrayal—how dare she get him to tell her all and then act coy about her own past, he asked her angrily. Whatever she told him after that made him realize how hopelessly trapped he was with that rakhi she had tied on his wrist to declare him a brother. His feelings now were not at all like a brother's towards a sister, he discovered.

'Don't you dare break that trust!' she warned him. 'That thread is the symbol of a sister's love for her brother and of his promise to protect her honour all his life!'

Sorry, the hero replied. All's fair in love and lust and I promise you I will look after you all my life if you will allow me to touch you 'like that'. I promise on the gods of my village I will never renege on this.

Then he leapt to feel her under the table that was strewn with her maths homework, and groped to find the satisfaction he sought.

When T'ta finished this tale, I told him in a disgusted voice that I was not like that at all.

'I am a writer,' I declared virtuously. 'In any case, there is nothing of this nature between Miss Yen and me and how dare you compare my relationship with her with your own sick past! Tell me,' I went on, 'if you took advantage of one student in Lahore, how can I believe that you haven't taken advantage of Miss Yen? So this is why you won't let me meet her—because you nurture secret longings for her yourself and are afraid that she will choose me over you, you old, sick man! You are jealous of my youth!' I declared with great satisfaction.

'I don't see any signs of youthful passion in you,

Mr Joshi,' T'ta replied. 'If you were really in the throes of youthful passion, believe me, you would have eloped with Miss Yen by now. You are just a writer,' he threw the word at me like an epithet. 'You write of what others do, Mr Joshi. And I know that one day you will write about all the stories I have told you. In fact, this is why I told them to you in the first place,' he said smugly.

So I decided to ask him about his secret longings for Miss Yen.

T'ta cleared his throat self-importantly. 'Mr Joshi,' he said finally, 'in the matter of sexual longings, I am younger than all of you young people. That is why I don't keep my wife near me, because if I have a woman in my bed, I can think of nothing else. This wastes my time and ruins my health. But, unlike depraved people like you, Mr Joshi, I don't expend my sexual energy on any woman who crosses my path. I just don't understand how you can call yourself a writer, Mr Joshi, if you have no respect for women. I worship women, Mr Joshi, and that is why—like a true worshipper— unless I love someone deeply, I do not move into action. So how can I do anything with Miss Yen if she considers me to be some kind of a father figure?'

'But suppose she starts to look at you as a lover,' I suggested wickedly, 'what then?'

'That's a separate matter, Mr Joshi. You can't even begin to imagine what I can do for the woman I love! Don't forget that I even broke my promise to a rakhi sister for love. I am the ultimate lover, Mr Joshi, a maha Majnu! What do they call it in Ingliss? A Great Lover. That's what I am!'

He refused to answer any questions about this Lahore woman: Did she still live there? Did he write to her? That she was an ugly ogress, I had no doubt now. So I decided that the next time T'ta scurried towards the forest after collecting his mail from the postman, I would tail him.

As luck would have it, a letter arrived three days later. I furtively followed him down the path to the forest and watched him read the letter. T'ta took it carefully out of the envelope, read the single sheet of paper closely, and sighed deeply. Then, he carefully folded it, put it back in the envelope and stashed it away in the inner pocket of his coat. After he had done this, he walked briskly towards Kalawati Yen's house.

I followed him, taking care to hide my movements, and was amazed to discover that he was sitting in the patch of green outside Kalawati's house and dictating something in a very low voice to her. Hidden from him, crouched behind a hedge some distance from them, all

I could make out was that Kalawati was taking down a letter T'ta was dictating to a woman called 'Premo'. At the end, when he came to the 'for ever and ever yours' bit, the name of the sender was 'Shashi'. He took the letter from Kalawati, read it through, looked around him, then took an envelope from the outer pocket of his coat. He put his reply inside it, sealed it and gave it to Kalawati, saying that it was to be sent to the usual address in Delhi. Kalawati wrote down the address and then hid the letter in a book. After this, T'ta started his English lessons with her.

I was waiting to greet him when he emerged from Kalawati's house.

'Hats off to you, sir!' I began. 'This is what they call killing two birds with one stone! By making her write a letter to your old lover, you just set the trap for catching a new one!' T'ta looked pale as he heard my voice, then quickly bustled me away to his secret place.

This is where he told me the whole story of his love affair with Prempyari. She could not even pronounce his name correctly, so on their journey towards the Main Point, she gave him a new one: Shashi. This was also the name of a girlfriend she had, so if she ever said 'I love Shashi and she loves me', no one would raise a finger.

As for T'ta, this new feminine identity meant that he could continue writing to her even after she was married: all he had to do was to find some unsuspecting girl with a feminine writing and get her to write the letters he dictated. As no girl he asked ever refused the pleas of this Great Lover, T'ta always managed to find someone or the other who willingly agreed to help out.

Then all hell broke loose: T'ta reached the Main Point with Prempyari and she promptly became pregnant. So she was forced to abort her foetus and was married off hurriedly to an indigent clerk by the 'uncle' she lived with. T'ta, on the other hand, was ignominiously thrown out of his benefactor's home and kicked out of Lahore. On his return, T'ta declared that he was a revolutionary who had to leave Lahore because he was in danger of being arrested. Once again, Bubu came to his rescue and sent him off to Sunaulidhar, to live in her house there and bide his time. He started teaching the village children in order to earn some money and, later, this developed into the village's primary school, thanks to the land and money donated by Pan Singh Bisht.

Now that I had heard the whole sordid story of T'ta's love affair with Prempyari, I felt so nauseated that I could not get myself to write of him or his love life. I was no longer amused by this affair between T'ta and Prempyari and all I could summon for his Great Lover persona was disgust and irritation.

The truth was that I was beginning to get tired of Sunaulidhar and this Fools' Paradise. I had fought with the principal, cursed Kalawati after her father complained about me to the school manager, and fought with the manager as well. It was at this point that someone came from T'ta's village to inform him that his family-planning methods had failed, his wife was pregnant and that he was needed there.

T'ta was miserable and I could not resist adding to his misery. I pointed out to him that Kalawati's complaint about me was made to the manager and not to T'ta. 'This means,' I added, 'that she has defected to the manager's camp, sir!'

Yet, nothing seemed more important to T'ta than the fact that if coitus interruptus had failed him, how would he ever control his sexual energy? Remember that contraceptives were not freely available then, and not available at all in the kind of remote villages that T'ta lived in. So I advised him to go in for a vasectomy.

He had been told of this by a doctor friend of his, he told me. Then why have you never considered it, I asked him.

T'ta was silent for a while. Then, after a long, thoughtful pause, he said, 'I think you should know, Mr Joshi, that both Prempyari and her husband are Arya Samajis and are childless.'

'What does all this have to do with your getting a vasectomy done, sir?' I asked in a puzzled voice.

'I have always given Premo every kind of help and support, Mr Joshi,' he replied. 'I've never let her down, never! When her husband failed to find something to do after they came to Delhi at the time of Partition, I contacted an old revolutionary friend of mine and got Premo trained as a typist, found her a job and helped out with money when she needed it. So I don't want that I should fail her if she ever wants a child. I can't tell her I can't help you because I have got myself vasectomized, can I? I tell you, the sacrifices one has to make for love, Mr Joshi, are really hard!'

When I went next to Almora for my summer break, I promptly told Lalit about the latest episode in the adventures of T'ta. Some progressive Urdu writers had started writing pretty explicitly about sex by then, but both Lalit and I agreed that there was something inherently distasteful about that genre. Soon after this, I was sent a letter by the school's manager terminating my tenure at the Sunaulidhar school, and the saga of T'ta and the Paradise of Fools ended there. I went off to Lucknow and from there to Delhi and somehow never found an opportunity to say a proper goodbye. So he vanished from my life along with the two porn titles I had lent him.

Some fifteen years later, this unfinished story was resurrected when I received a visitor's card from a Y.C. Pant, who worked for some shipping company and wanted to see me. It turned out that this YC was none other than T'ta's son Yatish, whom T'ta had once dreamed of sending to Oxford. I learnt from YC that he never went to Oxford because after he passed out of school (with very poor marks, I may add), he ran away to Bombay where he became a cabin boy, who started out by sweeping and swabbing the decks. That is how he reached America and eventually rose to become an officer with the shipping company. Later, he married an American girl and became an American citizen.

By the time I met Yatish, old memories had ceased to engage me very deeply—in fact, I blotted them out because they reminded me of my advancing years. Anyway, I spent a long time chatting with him and listening to his life story just as I had once chatted with his father. I was rather perturbed to hear that T'ta had permanently left Sunaulidhar and settled down in the plains, at a place near the town of Pilibhit. I found it impossible to imagine Sunaulidhar without T'ta or T'ta without Sunaulidhar.

'I had been pestering my father to stop working for some time,' YC told me. 'I once asked him to visit me in America but he refused. I used to send him money from there, to ease his life, but he stashed it all in a bank. Finally, I used that money and added some more to buy him a small farm near Pilibhit so that he could pass his days farming. But he chose to open a school instead, to educate the sons of the rich farmers of the region. How long will you keep working, I scolded him,' went on YC, 'but now I feel perhaps he was right. My mother passed away a few years ago, my sisters are all married, and I am in America. If it hadn't been for that school, he would have been a very lonely old man.'

YC finished his coffee and rose to leave. I politely saw him to the door and asked him casually about

Kalawati Yen. 'Do you remember that Chinese teacher,' I asked him, 'the one I gave maths lessons to? What happened to her?'

'Miss Yen? She remembers you all the time, sir, and you don't even remember her name!' he chided me, smiling as he did. 'She is a teacher in my father's school now.'

I couldn't help asking the next question: 'Does her husband also stay there?'

'She's not married, sir,' YC said. 'Would I call her Miss Yen if she were?'

He left after this but I was suddenly overcome with great nostalgia for that lost time. I was even a bit jealous of T'ta, the sly old fox who had succeeded where I had failed with Kalawati. Anyway, I shrugged off that memory, tore YC's card into two and chucked it into the wastepaper basket, aware that he had written down T'ta's present address at the back for me. T'ta was not a tragic or comic figure fit for a novel, I had decided: he was just good enough for a feature in a magazine. His story was no different from that of thousands of people who made good in the seventies—I myself was one of them. I had catapulted from being an ordinary school teacher to becoming an editor of a magazine just as T'ta had become the owner of a school from being a mere teacher. So, some months later, when a young freelance writer from Haldwani begged me to let him write something for my magazine, I asked him to do a feature on the nouveau riche farmers of the Terai area of my home state. Do an interview with T'ta, I told him, who runs a school for the children of rich farmers somewhere near Pilibhit. He never did. What is more, he cursed me publicly for pushing him into writing popular features rather than something more solid and creative.

Perhaps I had suggested the topic to him and made T'ta the subject of a magazine feature rather than the hero of a novel because I had recently moved to journalism from creative writing. In fact, I earned more kudos as a journalist than I had ever earned as a writer. So my past had a stamp of literariness and my future looked towards eminence. My present was dedicated to strengthening my position. I had reached an age when I had achieved the success that I sought, and the catty remarks of a hack from Haldwani did not shake my complacence. Yet, perhaps it was because of the malicious jealousy of people like him that I fell prey to a terrible bout of depression, so bad that I had to turn to a doctor for help.

In my depressed state, all those stories that T'ta had told me came back to haunt me and they did nothing to lighten my dark mood. In my present state of mind, he appeared to me not as a comic but as a deeply tragic figure, brought up in a house of widows and doomed to suffer the indignity of a village schoolmaster's life. To me, the real comic character of the saga was the young teacher-writer, namely, myself, who could not make a go of any relationship: he had no wife, no lover, no girlfriend or rakhi sister. I began to see how my failure was rooted in a sort of moral cowardice, and a proof of this was that each time I related the story of T'ta's sexual attraction to Kalawati Yen to my friends in Almora, I slyly censored my own feelings for her. Nor could I ever muster up the courage to confess my love for her: I took shelter behind other people's poems, or lyrics that others had written.

To me, now, the whole world appeared to be a paradise of fools, even if they were not all moral cowards like me. I felt that the comic-erotic was a cosmic tragedy—it affects each and every one of us, every day of our lives. To be born is to suffer, I reflected gloomily. Thus, born in 'The House of Widows', the earnest scholar of English in 'Hocus-Pocus', the intellectual of 'The Main Point', and the poor man's Casanova in 'Coitus Interruptus'—Professor Khashtivallabh, alias T'ta—now appeared to me to be the protagonist of a cosmic tragicomedy. My heavy heart told me that now that he had a school of his own and his son had become an American citizen, T'ta had become an even more tragic figure. I carefully went over all his stories and they appeared terribly depressing to me. I began to see in them an ingrained tragedy, a sort of Sisyphean situation, and found myself too cowardly and timid to address its fundamental pain.

So I decided to at least write 'Coitus Interruptus' as a short story, because that appeared to me the most touching of all T'ta's tales. Prempyari and T'ta's story was fit not just for guttersnipes but was part of an omnipresent, tragic universe. I felt that the mortal and temporal could be fused by some metaphysical sleight of hand to prove that even the most banal love stories have the potential of noble resolutions. However, I could never get myself to write 'Coitus Interruptus', because the death wish that arose from my depression would constantly interrupt me. In my neurotic state I'd set aside my pen and grope for my pulse instead and desperately seek a doctor. And when I had been calmed down with tranquillizers, I still could not go on because in my unstable emotional state, each word, each line, appeared so full of pathos that my eyes filled up with tears.

It was hopeless, whichever way I tried I just could not put down the plot that was ringing in my head. The naked tragedy of T'ta's life defeated me, both as a writer and as a person.

What is more, I felt I had to be totally honest and put down each episode with complete fidelity. I believed that if I could not do that, I would be guilty of a hideous crime. One false word, a false memory, and the delicate balance of the tragic tale would be tipped in another direction. For instance, in the scene where he discovers that Prempyari is pregnant and that a midwife has been summoned to quickly perform an illegal abortion, T'ta and Prempyari had escaped to a dark shed where coal and wood were stored. While she was giving him a blow job, T'ta had his eyes glued to the hole in the curtain and looked out anxiously. Did he say he saw the midwife or was it the candyfloss seller? To me it became crucial to remember this detail correctly, because the tragedy of the whole story hinged critically on it.

I became alarmed at my neurotic behaviour and ran to see a psychoanalyst, who prescribed some drugs that ended both my illness and the tragedy of T'ta's life story.

So that day, when the junior clerk of Sunaulidhar school called out from the bus and asked me to write about T'ta, I began to wonder whether I should try my hand at 'The House of Widows' once more. In fact, when I returned to Delhi, I rang up an editor friend and told him that I was creating the mood to write him a short story, and he was delighted.

Sadly, I found that I was unable to write the story when I sat down at my desk. At first I felt I had lost the immediacy of the plot, for what circulated now in my mind was the memory of a memory. It was as if I had once stuffed a whole video recording in my head but somehow the original print had got erased and only a scratchy copy of it remained. Like all scratchy copies, nothing was clearly visible any more and the dialogue was muffled and out of sync. The characters spoke in Hindi but it was not Hindi I heard now: It was as if I was watching a foreign film with bad Hindi subtitles. Also, some crucial scenes were missing. For instance, when he saw Boju's virgin blood on his kurta in the moonlight, had Lala wiped the blood with his kurta or did it stain on its own? And then there were some scenes that I could not remember from the original print: For instance, I could now see Boju grind some wild herbs to make a chutney for Lala. Was this in the original script or had I transposed it to the story after I saw a similar scene in Satyajit Ray's classic film, *Pather Panchali*?

Another frightening discovery was that I had lost not just the original plot but also the style and way of writing that would make it come alive. Once, I could suddenly stop at a point in media res, build up a scene and then abruptly change the pace, and accelerate to a pitch that left the reader breathless. Now, I stumbled badly at every turn.

I had lost it all: the plot, the style and even the writer who was confident he could create a comic satire out of someone's tragedy; the writer who once tore to shreds a story called 'The Chowkidar's Son' because he knew he could do better one day. I anticipated what the critics would say, and when I saw them peep over my shoulder at every word I put down, I lost all my self-confidence. I would never be able to pronounce the last verdict on T'ta, or use his immortal tragedy to confer something permanent on my reputation as a writer.

I was stuck, and my editor friend thought I was playing games with him because I had secretly planned to give the story to his rival. I swore this was untrue but I could see he did not believe me. He said, I'll only believe you when I have the story in my hands. So I sent off a letter to T'ta, at an address I concocted from memory, saying I want to write about Sunaulidhar and our time there, particularly about you because you were the most important person in my life then. Truth to tell, you were the most unforgettable character I ever met in my life, but I find I have forgotten many of the stories you told me, so I am attaching a questionnaire along with this letter. Please send it to me when you have completed it.

Some weeks later, the letter came back to me with 'Addressee Unknown' stamped on the envelope. So now my story had no protagonist and no writer. The person who once wrote it out mentally between bouts of laughter, shared with his friends in Almora, was lost forever. I had many excuses for not writing it, among them this: that if T'ta had replied and filled up my questionnaire, I could have tried to exhume the dead writer inside me. But that writer had been killed off by the anti-depressants that I was fed now. And if T'ta had replied to my letter, I would have at least known what I used to be in those faraway days. I was as perturbed by the discovery of my writer's block as I was by T'ta's second entry in my life. His tragedy reminded me of my own, and a terrible sadness threatened to turn my recovery into retreat. Desperate to keep him out of my mind, I turned my attention furiously towards putting together a special issue on ghosts and mystery tales.

∾

I was going through the final proofs of the issue when I got news that some distant relative of ours had passed away in the trans-Jamuna area and that I was to go there immediately as I was the oldest member of my clan in Delhi and someone had to represent our family at the funeral. This wasn't the best piece of news to receive at a time when I was battling with terminal depression, but I had to go. I schooled my face to the right expression of compassion and sadness and got ready to meet the dead man's family. I managed to mumble a few words of commiseration to the young son of the deceased, who was studying in class twelve, stroked his head gently and allowed him to wet my shirt-front with his tears. Then I turned to the widow, held her hand and mutely indicated that if they needed any money, I could help.

Then the dead man's boss arrived and, as an elder of the clan and an important person, I was taken aside to sit with him. I gravely accepted his condolences on behalf of the grieving family, even though I had had hardly any contact with them recently, and said that I hoped he would do something to help the family. The boss assured me that they would do all they could to release his pension funds as soon as possible and try and see if his widow could be given some sort of employment in his place. What happened to the poor man, the boss asked me solicitously, and I gave a graphic account of the fatal heart attack that had carried him off, with a total disregard for my own mental health.

I was looking for a way in which I could avoid going to the cremation grounds but again, as an elder of the clan, I had to go. Thankfully, someone else had taken charge of the rituals there, so on the excuse of making a vital phone call, I left the house hoping that I could avoid accompanying the funeral procession. I managed to delay my arrival at the cremation until the pyre had been lit, so I sauntered away to the river bank and lit a cigarette at a respectful distance from the burning pyre, watching the sluggish flow of the river. I pulled out a handkerchief to put against my nose to shield it from the noxious stench from the dirty water, when, suddenly, a voice behind me said, 'Sir, why are you standing here? There is a hand-pump and shade near the temple over there.'

I turned around and saw a young man who, I remembered, had been an enthusiastic participant in the rituals prior to the cremation. No, no, this is fine, I said. I couldn't tell him that the filthy, smelly river was a darn sight better than smelling the smoke of the funeral pyre. I thought he would leave but he hovered at a respectful distance.

Then, he cleared his throat and began, 'Sir, I've wanted to meet you for a very long time. My name is Jaydutt and I have an interest in reading and writing. In fact, I've published a few articles in local papers. I had once even requested Khashtivallabh-ji to send you some poems I had written, with a letter of recommendation. . .'

'Which Khashtivallabh-ji is this?' I interrupted.

'He was the owner of the school I attended, sir. Perhaps you knew him as Professor T'ta. He used to tell us how close you both were.'

'*Was* the owner?' I asked. 'What do you mean?'

'Oh, he passed away some time ago, sir. Before he died, he often spoke of you and told me how the junior clerk and principal of the Sunaulidhar school had told him that you had written a couple of stories about him. They used to pull his leg about it, sir, and tell him where they had seen it. But when he got the issue from

Haldwani or Nainital, he could never find them. He told me over and over again that I know Mr Joshi will definitely write about me one day because he knows the story of my whole life and understands that I am not an ordinary man. By the way, where exactly did you publish that story, sir?' he asked.

I had been standing with the burning pyres behind me, up to this point. Suddenly I felt as if a fresh pyre had been set alight inside me. Professor T'ta, that immortal character of my most important unwritten novel, had died before I had even created him.

I stood with my head bowed, unable to meet the young man's eyes. Finally, I asked him in a feeble voice, 'When was this? What happened to him?'

'He died over five years ago, sir,' I was told. 'He had a massive heart attack on the first death anniversary of his son Yatish, and just dropped dead. They say he died of a broken heart, although he never breathed a word of his sorrow to any living soul as long as he was alive. Not even when his only son committed suicide. No one ever saw him shed a tear, but occasionally he used to mutter, "Why? Why?" in English to himself.'

I could not get myself to ask him any more. But the fellow went on with his story—in this age of moving pictures, who can resist the person who is willing to listen to a long-winded tale? The death of a grieving father—a phrase like this alone makes the entire story flash before one's eyes. Who needs words any more? And who has the patience to either say or hear more than this?

Despite this, that heartless poet went on with his tale. Yatish had a huge row with his American wife. She divorced him and fought and won a bitter custody battle over their son. The court accepted her testimony that Yatish was a mentally sick person with homosexual tendencies and so not fit to bring up their son. Then she went and married her lover, I was told. Yatish returned to his father and decided to start life afresh with him. He bought some more land for a farm and invested in a tractor. His father tried to persuade him to marry Miss Yen although she was older by about six, seven years. T'ta told them both that they were the two people he loved most in this world and that his deepest desire was to see them married and rear a family before he died. They agreed to humour his wish and then, on the morning of their wedding day, when Miss Yen took Yatish his morning cup of tea, she could not get him to open the door.

'So I was summoned, sir,' the poet went on relentlessly, 'and when I peeped in over the ledge outside his window, I saw Yatish's body swinging from the ceiling fan. I cannot tell you how revolting it was, sir!' he shuddered at the memory.

I tried to stop him from saying any more but he was not going to spare me the gory details of the hanging corpse.

'Yatish's tongue had popped out, sir, and shit had stained his clothes. Why do you think a foreign-returned man like Yatish would adopt such a crude way of death?' he asked me now. 'Was it because he could not confront his father and Miss Yen with his homosexuality? Or was he appalled at marrying the woman his father had had a sexual relationship with?'

Neither of us knew the answers.

'The school and farm are now with Miss Yen,' he went on, undeterred by my silence. 'T'ta had named her his legal heir, you see. She is married now to the local bank clerk,' he added slyly, 'and some people say that Yatish's suicide may not have been a suicide after all. You knew her quite well, sir, do you think this could be true, sir?'

I could not say anything and he seemed bent on getting a reaction from me. Thankfully, someone called out that the logs on the pyre needed readjusting, and he bustled off self-importantly to fix things there.

I turned my unseeing gaze to the river once more.
All I was aware of was that what flowed past me was a
river and that it was filthy. A crow was perched on
something that floated and was tugging at it. The river
hardly moved and each time the crow tugged, he flapped
his wings to maintain his balance. What he was perched
on, I could not make out.

The poet returned once more, for the funeral was
finally over. 'What are you watching there, sir?' he
asked. 'It looks like some dead child's body. I'm sure it
is someone's illegitimate child,' he added in a disgusted
tone.

I looked carefully then, and he was right. The crow
was feasting on a dead foetus. Things blurred before me
and the cawing of the crow sounded, to me, like someone
calling: 'T'ta.'

I couldn't tear my gaze away: The dead child's
bloated body bobbing on the waves appeared to be
asleep. A crow was singing it a lullaby and the lullaby
had just two syllables: Kay-ne. Kay-ne. No-thing. Nothing.

'What are you staring at that corpse for, sir?' the
poet asked again. 'Tell me the story of T'ta's life, sir.
What did you know about him that we did not?'

I remained silent, for he would never understand

that what I was staring at was the substance of T'ta's life. I stared at it like a child looks at his hand—without disgust or understanding—when he has smeared it with his own shit.